The One
Left Behind

The One Left Behind

WILLO DAVIS ROBERTS

SCHOLASTIC INC.
New York Toronto London Auckland Sydney
Mexico City New Delhi Hong Kong Buenos Aires

No part of this publication may be reproduced, stored in a retrieval system, or transmitted in any form or by any means, electronic, mechanical, photocopying, recording, or otherwise, without written permission of the publisher. For information regarding permission, write to Atheneum Books for Young Readers, an imprint of Simon & Schuster Children's Publishing Division, 1230 Avenue of the Americas, New York, NY 10020.

ISBN-13: 978-0-545-03639-9
ISBN-10: 0-545-03639-9

12 11 10 9 8 7 6 5 4 3 2 1   7 8 9 10 11 12/0

Printed in the U.S.A.   40

First Scholastic printing, October 2007

Book design by Christopher Grassi
The text for this book is set in Berkeley Old Style.

≈ 1 ≈

Mandy had lived in this house for eleven years, all of her life, and she had never been afraid here before.

She was afraid now.

She used to sleep through the night, secure in knowing that her twin sister, Angel, was beside her in the big bed, and more often than not feeling the weight of Herry against her feet and smelling his familiar doggie aroma.

Tonight Mandy awoke in darkness, alone in the bed, for even Herry had deserted her. For a moment she didn't remember that Angel was gone, that she would not be coming back, and then the pain hit her like a physical blow. It knocked the wind out of her, and she made a protesting sound.

A moment later she heard the clicking of big toenails on

the wooden floor before they were softened by the rag rug, and the bear-sized nose nudged coldly at her outflung hand.

The dog whined, echoing her own misery.

"Where have you been?" Mandy demanded, and he whined again as he leaped onto the bed, nearly crushing her when his 120 pounds collapsed against her legs.

She answered her own question. "You're looking for her, aren't you?" Her hand crept down to fondle the shaggy fur, the ear that pricked up at the sound of her voice. "I keep looking for her too, Herry."

She swallowed hard, knowing it didn't matter if she spoke aloud to the dog. There was no one to hear her in the empty house.

"She's gone, you know. She's not coming back. Not ever."

She had thought she'd already cried all the tears her body could manufacture, but a few more leaked out and ran down the sides of her face, into her ears. It was a strange, uncomfortable sensation, and she lifted both hands to swipe at the moisture.

If she allowed herself to *really* cry, her nose would plug up so she couldn't breathe, and then she'd have a headache.

She reached for a tissue, blew her nose, and determined not to permit that to happen. "Let's pretend," she said to Herry, "that she's only downstairs getting a sandwich. That she's coming back to bed in a few minutes."

Herry made one of his comforting, deep-in-the-throat murmurs of agreement.

"Let's pretend what we'll all do tomorrow," Mandy proposed. "We'll go way up the beach, and I'll make up a story about a planet where everybody looks like you; all big and black and hairy, only they can speak. And Angel will be a princess, and I'll be the hero who goes out to rescue her from a strange tribe that has stolen her, and you can be the King of the Gigantic Dogs, okay?"

He poked once more at her hand, and she took another swipe at the tears that persisted in leaking, and deliberately fell into the world where she could control everything and her sister could not die.

Sometimes she pretended wonderfully well, and for a while she could be happy again. Of course she couldn't force herself to stay in that drifting world of fantasy, and soon she'd drop back into the darkness that threatened to smother her.

Back and forth, back and forth she would go. Remembering all the good times, making up her delightful adventurous stories, and sharing them with Angel, and acting them out to great hilarity. Just the two of them— and Herry—acting all the parts. Angel wasn't clever with dialogue or plots, but she was a wonderful actress, and she took direction well.

And then the curtain would fall, cutting off the fascinating ideas, and Mandy would choke up and cling to Herry, and the dog would try to absorb the sorrow that she thought would surely kill her, too.

She would heal herself by remembering, by making believe that everything remained the same as it had always been. That she and Angel were still a team, and they would go on having the fun kind of adventures they'd planned for the summer.

But deep down she knew it was all a lie. She did not have a magical ability to reestablish what had been, not anywhere except in her memory.

It occurred to her now, in the middle of the night in the huge silent house, that even if the entire family had been home, she would still be alone. She could not reach out and touch any of them, nor would it mean anything if she could.

Mandy had not intended to stay home all alone that weekend.

Everybody had asked her if she wanted to go with *them,* except for Mom and dad. They were celebrating their twenty-fourth wedding anniversary by staying in a hotel in Traverse City and sleeping late, going to some shows, eating dinner in the best restaurants, relaxing. They wanted to do it by themselves, no kids, and had left early to beat the traffic.

It was a three-day weekend and all the boys had plans.

Bert and Fairy had been married for only three months. They hadn't yet found a place of their own, and when they were home they went into Bert's room and closed the door, content with their own company. They were still on their honeymoon. This weekend they had opted to camp out somewhere on the beach. That didn't sound very exciting, since they already *lived* on the beach.

"You want to come with us, Mandy?" Bert asked. "I told Mom and Dad we'd take you."

She wouldn't have agreed anyway, even if she hadn't glimpsed Fairy's expression. *Fairy* certainly didn't want company in their tent.

Mandy was still getting used to Fairy. She called Bert "Bertie Baby," which sounded pretty silly from a grown-up woman. If any male had so addressed him, Bert would have knocked the guy's block off. Yet Mandy's oldest brother just grinned as if Fairy was the cleverest thing since electric lights.

"I don't know yet," Mandy said, knowing she'd never join them. "I might be going to Gus's tournament."

"You're welcome if you want to come," Bertie Baby assured her, not seeing his wife's horrified countenance behind him.

Bel was joining several buddies somewhere racing junker cars. "You want to come, Mandy?" he asked. "We're gonna sleep in our cars, and it'll be just guys, but—"

"No, thanks," Mandy said. It would be even worse than tenting with Bert and Fairy.

Dickon had just met a new girl. He'd been interested in a lot of girls during his nineteen years, but this one, he enthused, was really special. Striking, naturally. Dark hair and eyes, an incredible figure—everything a guy would want in a girlfriend.

To Mandy, with no hint of a figure to come in sight, the thought of meeting her was depressing. She was pretty well convinced that she'd never have a womanly shape.

"Her folks have this huge house on Gull Island. They're having a big house party for the whole weekend, starting Friday night. There'll be a mob, people all ages. She has a younger brother your age, Mandy. You could hang out with him."

"Bert and Fairy asked me to go camping," she said. She'd never enjoyed meeting new people, especially in crowds, and on an island, she couldn't even walk home if she wanted to.

Rude, at seventeen, was torn between an interest in girls and motorcycles. The bikes were safer; you didn't have to work up your courage to approach one, you didn't get tongue-tied in the presence of a cycle, and they were almost as exciting.

"Bud's folks are going to be gone," he said, "and we're going to be tearing apart that new bike he got. I'll just stay over there, instead of running back and forth, and we can work all night if we want to." His face turned pink, so Mandy guessed what was coming before he spoke. "His sister Heather's sixteen. Older than you are, but I asked if it would be all right if you came along and she said sure. You could hang out with her."

Mandy felt like an orphan. In spite of living in the middle of a big family, she was all alone without Angel. Still, if she didn't go meet Heather—she already knew Bud, a big gangly kid who only came to life when talking or riding motorcycles—what would she do this last weekend before school started?

She shrugged, leaving it up in the air.

Gus was going to be playing baseball all three days. He was a first baseman in a local league, and the playoffs were going to be held in Traverse City. His team would be driving over in a couple of vans.

"Some of the girls are going too. We're staying at some of the other teams' houses. They're all kids you know, Mandy."

Sure. Girls Gus's age, four years older. All they'd talk about, when they weren't watching the games, was boys and clothes and makeup.

"Umm. Maybe," she said.

A year ago, when Angel was still here, none of the boys would have invited her anywhere. She knew they did so now because they were sorry for her, not because they wanted her company. Angel had been their sister too, but they all knew it was worse for Mandy because Angel had been her twin.

None of the choices excited her. And then she got engrossed in a book, and when she came downstairs everybody was gone, except for Herry.

The Sebolds had left home in too many different vehicles, at various times. Even Uncle Frank had been picked up by his sister, Aunt Eileen, who had orders to make sure he took his meds while he was with her. Each group apparently assumed Mandy had decided to go with one of the others. Nobody was worrying about her.

To begin with, Mandy didn't worry either.

She had lived in this house for her entire life. There was nothing scary about it. She had Herry for company, padding silently at her side wherever she went, licking her hand from time to time. Even so, she knew she should call her parents. They would never allow her to stay alone so long.

Mandy went to the small desk in the kitchen, where the phone sat. Mom and Dad always left a number there, telling where they were and how they could be reached. Even if they only went grocery shopping, there was always a note. Not this time. All she found was a list in Mom's handwriting stating where each family member would be that weekend, with a check mark by each name. "Bert, Fairy, Mandy—camping," it said.

She tried to remember which hotel Mom and Dad had gone to, but she hadn't paid attention to their plans. Mandy knew how to reach Rude, but she still didn't want to hang out with his friend's sister while he fixed a motorcycle, nor did she want him to have to come home, as if she needed a babysitter.

The phone rang, startling her. "Mandy? It's Mrs. Turner, Nathan's mom. Thank goodness you're still there. Nathan's supposed to come over this weekend to feed Herry and let him out, but he's in the hospital. He had an emergency appendectomy this morning." The woman talked fast, not giving Mandy a chance to say anything. "I'm sorry to back out on you folks at the last minute; I know all of you are leaving, but it can't be helped."

She finally paused for breath and Mandy said, "I didn't go. There was a mix-up and—"

"Oh, good. Then you can take care of Herry and I won't worry any longer." And with that, she hung up.

Mandy decided to stay alone. There was plenty of food in the pantry and the freezer. She had a new stack of library books. And with no one to hear, she could talk to herself all she liked. It would be fun to stay alone. Wouldn't it?

2

Mandy stood in the kitchen, wondering what to do with her freedom. If Angel had been there, the weekend would soon be an adventure. Everything had been fun with Angel, and Mandy had been more daring with Angel to egg her on. Even at school.

The twins had quickly discovered that their teacher could not tell them apart, especially when they dressed alike, which they insisted on doing. When Mrs. Fletcher called on Mandy, she would glance toward Angel, and Angel would reply. Mandy almost always knew the correct answers, but she was painfully shy about speaking up in class.

Angel was not shy at all, except when she *didn't* know the answer. Then she would glance at Mandy, and somehow, when nobody could tell which of them was which, it was much easier for Mandy to speak up and sound confident.

The school in Suttons Bay, Michigan, was a small one, with only one class for each grade, so there was no practical way to split the twins up. They stuck together, defying the rest of the world. If anyone picked on one of them, the other was certain to join in to present a united front. That didn't mean that they didn't occasionally squabble between themselves. When Mandy wanted to pretend one thing, and Angel wanted to play something else, they sometimes went their separate ways. Herry would join whichever of them struck his fancy, looking like a bear in his dark thick coat, with his tail wagging whenever he was spoken to.

When Mama said, "Girls, it's time to set the table," she didn't care which of them obeyed the order. When she stated that it was time they cleaned their shared room, each of them would look at the other and say, "It's your turn." Sometimes they worked together, in the way that they played together. Most tasks were more quickly and easily done as a team.

Once in a while Mandy had a fleeting reflection that it would be nice to be thought of as an individual. Someone apart from her sister. She was convinced that Angel was smarter and prettier than she herself was, so she knew they were separate. Still, it would be nice to be considered as a single person by others.

When she said something to that effect, Mama laughed. "How can she be prettier when she looks exactly like you? Come on, both of you, carry out the trash so the boys can burn it when they get home."

Nobody knew all the really dangerous stuff they did. Angel always got the ideas, then talked Mandy into going along with her plans. The worst had been the day they took a vee-bottom boat out on the lake, pretending to be pirates, and the boat overturned in water over their heads. Mandy had been gasping for breath, heart pounding, when her fingers clutched the side of the "pirate ship."

Angel had just laughed. "You're such a chicken, Mandy."

She was, she supposed. It was almost always her sister who wanted to try something risky. And *she* was chicken enough to follow along rather than argue her sister out of it.

The boys at school couldn't resist needling the twins. While Mandy resented it when her hair was pulled, or she was tripped while passing down the aisle, or her pencil was stolen, her way of handling it was to pretend it hadn't happened, to ignore her tormenter.

Not so Angel. She wasn't above returning tit for tat: swinging around with a sharp elbow to jab it into someone's ribs, stomping on the foot that had been extended into her path, wrestling her pencil away from the thief. It didn't matter to her if they were on the playground or in the classroom; her retaliation was immediate. Sometimes that resulted in a trip to the office or a time-out session on a bench. Angel never seemed to care about possible consequences. She never backed down from a confrontation.

And if there were harsh words, Angel was quick with the comebacks that Mandy only thought of hours—or days—later. Comebacks that made the other kids laugh and defused the situation while at the same time humiliating the heckler. After a while it took a brave individual to provoke one of the twins deliberately. Mandy relied on Angel to handle the bullies.

And then Angel died.

She was ten years old, and she'd always been the best and the smartest and the prettiest. And she ate an undercooked hamburger that was tainted by E. coli, and she was rushed to the hospital, violently ill, and within two days she had died.

It wasn't possible.

Mandy refused to believe it. She tried to withdraw from the reality into make-believe, the way she had so often done to escape from any unpleasantness in the past, and for brief periods she managed to pretend that her sister was in the next room.

"Ten-year-olds don't die," she'd insisted, facing her

family with grief written on her face. "Not unless they're careless and step in front of a truck or something." On several occasions Angel had run across a street when there were cars coming, while Mandy had held back until the traffic had passed. But Angel had always escaped unharmed and waited on the far curb, laughing, for her sister to join her.

"Several other people got sick, too," Bel said. "It was in the paper. They all ate at Dilly's Deli, too."

"So did I," Mandy said, barely able to speak.

"But you didn't have a hamburger," Dickon pointed out. "You ate something different."

"A grilled cheese," Mandy remembered. "She had a hamburger, but I wanted grilled cheese that time."

None of the other victims died, though several were sick enough to be hospitalized for weeks.

Angel was buried in a white coffin, and everybody in town came except those who were still hospitalized, and Dilly's Deli was closed while the authorities investigated. Then the proprietor put a sign on the door that said, "Gone Out of Business." He couldn't bear the thought of anyone else being poisoned by his food.

And Mandy was no longer a twin. She was a single, and she felt as if more than half of herself had been torn away.

The color, the music, the joy went out of her life.

It was no longer possible to imagine herself out of a horrible experience. It no longer worked to pretend anything beautiful, or exciting, or magical. Without Angel to share, Mandy felt broken, destroyed.

How could her life already be over when she was only ten years old?

Yet how could she reshape her life into anything meaningful without her twin sister?

Herry was the only one who truly seemed to understand. He stuck closer to her side, his dark eyes fixed on hers, and he licked at her hand or her face with what she knew was heartbreak as severe as her own.

The entire family grieved, of course. At the funeral, beside the newly opened grave in the local churchyard, they all clung together and wept.

But now, nearly a year after the burial, everyone but Mandy seemed to have moved on. Mom had taken up her meetings and her normal activities. Dad returned to his duties at the hardware store, selling shovels and lawnmowers and mixing paint and handing out free advice about how to install a garbage disposal or replace a damaged lock. Uncle Frank puttered in the yard or went for long walks.

And the brothers took up their lives where they'd left off. Jobs, sports, girlfriends, hobbies.

Mandy didn't have a job. Except for swimming in the

bay and walking for miles at a stretch through the woods or along the sandy shore, she wasn't into sports. Her primary preoccupation had always been reading, but the books had lost their power to engulf her, to carry her away to other times and places.

And she had no friends.

That came as an additional shock when she realized it.

She had never felt the need for friends. She'd had Angel. They'd had all they needed in each other.

It wasn't that they were hostile toward other girls, or indifferent to them. They greeted others in a friendly manner. They were invited to birthday parties. But none of the other girls were used to including the twins in their ordinary, everyday plans. It was taken for granted that they were content to do things together, not needing anyone else.

After Angel died, Mandy sensed that the other girls were at a loss as to how to offer their sympathy. They didn't know what to say, so they said nothing at all. They avoided her so that they wouldn't have to think or speak about what had happened to her sister.

It wasn't that Mandy *wanted* to go skating or to the movies with other girls. As far as she knew, none of them were into making up stories or plays and acting them out. If they had fantasy lives, she'd never heard about them.

But she was so *alone*. Herry demonstrated that he, too,

was lonely, and he did his best to melt into her skin, to keep her company, but it wasn't enough.

Once school was out, when Mandy got up in the morning she had nothing to do after she'd eaten a banana and a bowl of cereal.

Not even her birthday had been fun that year. It should have been Angel's birthday, too. They should have blown out the eleven candles together.

Mandy tried harder to survive the only way she knew how: taking refuge in make-believe.

The easiest way was to pretend that her sister hadn't died at all. That she was somewhere else, out of sight, but would soon return. That they were going to come up with a new story idea and act it out.

She tried doing all the dialogue herself. She took all the parts, changing her voice when she switched from one character to another. And then one day she heard her mother talking to Uncle Frank.

"Frank, you've skipped your meds again, haven't you? You got into trouble at the Market. Mr. Adamson called me."

"I wasn't hurting anybody," Uncle Frank said. He was clenching and unclenching his hands.

"It makes people nervous when you talk to yourself out loud. And say weird things to people when you don't even know them. You created a disturbance and frightened Dolly Framer's mother-in-law."

"She's a stupid old cow," Uncle Frank said, scowling.

Mandy, listening, had to agree with him. She'd encountered Mrs. Framer at church and found her to be argumentative and overbearing.

"That doesn't mean you can be rude to her," Mom said.

"Wasn't rude. Just said the truth. She was squeezing the tomatoes, and I told her to stop, they don't like it. She told me to mind my own business, and I told her someone would punish her."

"That's not for you to decide. You might have told Mr. Adamson if she was damaging the fruit, and let him take care of it."

"He looks at me with evil eyes," Uncle Frank stated. "I don't like him. I can't trust him."

"Then it would be better if you stayed out of his store. Or better yet if you remembered to take your pills," Mom suggested.

The clenched fists suddenly smashed down on the counter, making Mandy jump. "I *hate* the meds! They make me feel crummy! I don't want to take them anymore."

Mom had stepped back a pace when he struck the counter, but her voice remained calm. "The agreement, Frank, was that if you were to live with us instead of in the home, you would take the medicine. You behave perfectly well as long as you take the pills. If you were ill with pneumonia, you would take antibiotics to make you well. This is the same thing."

"No, it ain't! I don't have pneumonia, and the pills don't make me well. They just cover up my mind, make me somebody I'm not. I'm not crazy, Bea! It's everybody else who's crazy, and they're all trying to make me think it's *me*!"

"I'll have to talk to Isaac, then. About sending you back to the home. We can't have you frightening people. We have a houseful of children, Frank."

"Your kids never been afraid of me," Frank stated, still scowling.

That was true. Uncle Frank said and did some odd things, but Mandy didn't think any of them had ever been afraid of him. He had never hurt anybody. It was embarrassing to be around him when he started a ruckus in a public place, though. Almost everybody in Suttons Bay knew Uncle Frank was schizophrenic, and if he did anything bizarre it meant he'd neglected to take his prescribed medications. They called Mom or Dad if the behavior was too far out.

Frank suddenly noticed Mandy standing in the doorway. "Who are you?" he demanded, still speaking fiercely.

"Mandy," she said.

"The real one, or the pretend one?" The question

didn't make any sense, of course. Sometimes what Uncle Frank said didn't. But the answers didn't necessarily have to make sense either.

"The real one," Mandy said.

He grunted. "I thought so. You're not afraid of me, are you?"

"No," Mandy said, glancing obliquely at her mother to see if she'd object to that.

"Just because I was talking to those tomatoes that old woman was pinching doesn't mean I need to be locked up, does it? Because a man talks to himself doesn't make him crazy, does it? When what the other people are saying doesn't make any sense?"

"No," Mandy said.

Mom drew in a deep breath. "Either you take the pills the way you're supposed to, Frank, or Isaac and I will have to discuss making different living arrangements for you."

"Who are you?" Frank demanded, glaring at her.

"I'm Beatrice, your sister-in-law. As you know perfectly well." Mom's face was turning a bit pink.

"You *look* like Bea. You have her face. But you're an imposter," Frank declared. "My enemies do that sometimes, hide behind a mask, pretending to be my friends."

He turned abruptly away from both of them and headed out the back door, letting the screen slam behind him.

Now it was Mom whose hands were clenched. "I ought to know better than to argue with him. Maybe your father can get him back on the pills."

"He never hurts anybody," Mandy said.

"Not so far. But he's so far off-base he might."

Mandy hesitated. "It bothers people when he talks to himself, especially if he gets loud when he's in the store. But talking to yourself isn't exactly . . . crazy, is it?"

Mom picked up a dishcloth and began to clean the counter. "No, of course not. Everybody talks to themselves once in a while. Mandy, go down in the cellar and get me a couple of quarts of blueberries, will you? I think I'll make a cobbler for supper."

"I love blueberry cobbler," Mandy murmured as she headed down the stairs. And then realized she was talking to herself, just like Uncle Frank.

When Angel was alive, they'd talked mostly to each other. But she couldn't remain silent all the time now, and nobody else was interested in what she had to say about anything.

If she talked to herself, did that mean she was schizophrenic too? Or was it only if you talked to tomatoes and were rude to strangers?

She wasn't very much like Uncle Frank. Even when she voiced her thoughts aloud, when she was alone, they made sense. She didn't think people were trying to trick her by hiding behind masks, pretending to be someone else.

She decided that the next time she was alone, when nobody would ask what she was looking up, she would see what she could find out about being schizophrenic. She didn't foresee that she would be quite so completely alone, though, when she had a chance to look up the problem.

≈ 3 ≈

She was still halfway in denial that Angel was gone. She pretended that her sister was going to appear any moment with a suggestion for some adventure or game.

It was hard to keep up that pretense, though, as she and Herry walked through the empty rooms. There were no voices, no laughter. No music.

The conviction came suddenly, crushing her with the pain of it.

Angel was dead. She was never coming back. And Mandy herself was never going to have that joyful and comforting presence in her life again.

"I can't stand it," she said aloud into the silence. "How can I be only *half* of what I was before? Why didn't I get a hamburger, like she did, instead of a toasted cheese, and die too?"

Her voice was too loud. Herry nudged her hand, and she obediently scratched behind his ear. The big dog leaned heavily against her leg, almost knocking her over.

"Is talking to you the same as talking to myself?" she wondered. "Mom says everybody talks to themselves once in a while, but people look at you funny if they see you doing it. Some of them get all upset when they hear Uncle Frank. He's not *crazy*. He's sick. Only not everybody can tell the difference."

She went into Dad's den and knelt down in front of the bookcase where he kept the reference books. Dictionaries, encyclopedias, books about diet and health. She pulled out a thick red paperback. *The Merck Manual of Medical Information*. Wouldn't it be in that one?

She had trouble locating it because she wasn't sure how to spell schizophrenia. She finally found it, sitting flat on the floor with Herry's nose resting against one of her crossed legs.

"Schizophrenia and delusional disorder." That sounded like Uncle Frank, all right. Having delusions meant believing things that weren't true, didn't it? Like Uncle Frank thinking some evil stranger was hiding behind a mask that looked like Mom. Or that Mr.

Adamson, who had six grandchildren he spoiled rotten, looked at him with evil eyes.

She read the words aloud. "'Schizophrenia is a major mental disorder of unknown cause, typically characterized by a separation between the thought processes and the emotions, a distortion of reality accompanied by delusions and hallucinations, a fragmentation of the personality, motor disturbances, bizarre behavior—'"

Mandy paused. "That's Uncle Frank. Bizarre behavior, talking to tomatoes in the grocery store, being rude to people—" When Herry nudged her leg, she remembered to continue stroking his head. Herry was suffering too, she thought. He missed Angel as much as she did, he just couldn't say anything about it. She had tried to explain to him that her sister had become ill from eating tainted meat, and died, but she knew he couldn't really understand anything except grief that she wasn't there.

She smoothed the pages on her lap and continued reading. The text listed some medications that were used in schizophrenic patients. She wasn't sure what Uncle Frank took—when he could be persuaded to swallow the pills. One of the things listed was lithium for manic-depressive symptoms. Was that Uncle Frank?

It said that lithium could cause serious toxic side effects.

Uncle Frank said the medicines made him feel rotten.

Did it make sense to take medication that stopped you from talking to tomatoes and convinced you that your relatives weren't evil strangers hiding behind masks, but made you feel sick in some other way?

She remembered taking an antibiotic once that made her sick to her stomach. The cure was worse than the disease she was taking it for.

Mandy bit her lip and bent forward to hug Herry. "Maybe you're lucky you're a dog and you don't understand anything."

He licked her ear until she withdrew from him and continued reading. "'Characterized by withdrawing from reality and thinking in illogical, confused patterns. Developing delusions and behaving as if in a fantasy world. They may hear voices, maybe messages from God.'"

It might be comforting to hear messages from God, Mandy thought. Even if you didn't really hear them, it might be reassuring to *think* you did.

Mandy wondered what Uncle Frank had said to the tomatoes.

She read some more, struggling over the big words but getting the gist of what the book had to say about what was the matter with Uncle Frank. He couldn't help the way he was. For the most part he was not dangerous, though strangers often perceived that he was, and taking the drugs the doctors wanted him to take made him feel so horrible he'd rather be thought insane than deal with the unpleasant side effects.

Finally she closed the book and slid it back into the bookcase.

There were a lot of things in life that didn't seem to have any satisfactory answers or solutions.

Mandy sighed. "Come on, Herry, let's take a walk."

Herry never turned down that invitation.

Summer was almost over, but it was still warm and sunny. There was enough of a breeze to turn up a few whitecaps on the bay, and the water wasn't too cold to wade in as she turned away from town.

There were houses in that direction, and that meant people. She wasn't in the mood to encounter people.

In the other direction, Mrs. Hodge's cottage had stood deserted since the old lady passed away. And beyond that, nothing but empty beach and eventually the lighthouse that was no longer used, out on the end of the point.

When they were together, the twins had almost always chosen to go in the direction of isolation. Usually they'd been making up some story, acting it out, or playing some game.

Mandy tried, but it wasn't fun without her sister. The ideas wouldn't even come. Mandy didn't remember when she'd ever run out of ideas before. Without Angel to spark them and elaborate upon them, the part of her that generated imagination seemed to have expired.

Walking beside the water had always had a soothing effect on her, but today the tranquility wouldn't come. Maybe if she just got tired enough, Mandy thought, she could go home and sleep. If she was lucky, she wouldn't even dream about anything sad. Sometimes Angel was still there, laughing, teasing, full of joy, in her dreams.

Mandy walked farther than she'd really intended, all the way to the lighthouse that stood tall against the sky. She'd always liked the lighthouse, but today is seemed shabby and forlorn, with no light and no foghorn to warn boats away from the rocky shore.

The lighthouse was supposed to be locked up, but long ago Angel had pried the boards off the nailed-up door and climbed to the top of the tower. When Mandy followed, she had fallen through a rotted wooden platform, catching herself by her elbows and scraping them badly. Unwilling to explain how she'd been injured, the girls had sneaked back into the house and foraged for first aid supplies. Mandy had worn long-sleeved shirts until the scabs healed.

Although the lighthouse made her nervous after that, Mandy and Angel had spent many hours there, climbing the circular stairway, risking falling through rotting flooring. Herry always waited below, refusing to attempt the iron steps, perhaps wiser than they were.

The view from the top was exhilarating, but today Mandy was not tempted. Always before, the girls had known that if there was an accident and one of them was hurt, the other one would run to get help.

Knowing that help was available if needed made a big difference in what seemed reasonable to do. Knowing there was no help made her wary now.

It was late afternoon when Mandy and Herry headed back toward home, walking, as usual, on the hard-packed sand next to the water. She glanced at Mrs. Hodge's abandoned cottage and wondered if anybody would ever live in it again, or if it would eventually fall down because nobody cared enough about it to repair anything.

The dock had already begun to disintegrate. Nobody had used it for years, not since Mrs. Hodge's grandchildren had grown up and moved away and stopped coming to visit. If Angel had still been there, they might have taken some of the boards that were falling into the water and built something out of them. A shack, a castle, a boat maybe?

Mandy was almost past the sagging structure when she realized she was seeing something out of the ordinary. On a beach where nobody but the Sebold twins had spent any time in years, favoring instead the public beach in town where there was a lifeguard and playground equipment, there was a footprint.

A very small footprint.

Mandy stopped, staring at it.

A small, bare footprint right on the edge of the bay.

Herry, sensing her interest, came up to her and nuzzled her hand, and she grabbed his collar and pulled him aside. "Don't step on it, Herry! It's a little kid. A little kid, practically a baby, was walking here!"

A sweeping glance in a 360-degree turn gave her no clues. The bay was empty of boats. The beach, as far as she could see, to their own dock another quarter of a mile away, was devoid of movement. Nobody at the edge of the woods. Nobody around the deserted cottage.

"Nobody'd let a little kid that size walk around alone, this close to the water." Herry was pressed against her leg, and she absently fondled his ears. "I don't think there were any footprints when we went by on the way out to the point, were there?"

It was lucky Herry was a good listener, or she'd be talking to herself. Mandy spun again, putting her own foot alongside the smaller one. "I hope he didn't go into the water."

Last summer a child had drowned just beyond the edge of the public beach in town, in spite of supposedly being watched by a mother, a grandmother, and two older sisters.

Mandy's heartbeat quickened. It had been a terrible thing, and she hoped that no child had been in danger here.

Only a few feet from the waterline the loose sand showed no trace of other footprints. Surely there had been an adult here, who had rescued the little one who had made the tiny print. It was impossible to tell.

Uncertainly, she waded out into the bay, looking down through the clear water. There were a few stones on the sandy bottom. If there had been anything else, she would have seen it.

"There's no sign of anybody here now," she told Herry, who watched from the shore as she walked back to him. "Anybody with that small a foot couldn't have taken a very big step. You'd think there'd be more than one footprint."

Herry was a satisfactory companion. He never disputed her conclusions. Of course he never helped figure out any of the answers, either.

Frowning a little, giving up, Mandy went on around the shore end of the dock and then stopped again.

An old broom had been dropped beside the decking, and she could clearly see where it had been used to sweep across the damp sand.

Why would anyone sweep the beach? Sometimes, at the park on the edge of town, the kids who took turns being lifeguards would clean the sand of cigarette butts and other trash with one of those fine-toothed rakes, but never with a broom.

Except for the Sebolds—mainly the twins—it was rare that anyone ever came here. They were all scrupulous about cleaning up after themselves. Mom and Dad had drilled into them all their lives to pick up their trash.

Mystified, Mandy contemplated the broom. She supposed it was no business of hers.

"Come on, let's go home and get something to eat," she told the dog. And Herry, recognizing the word "eat," wagged his tail with enthusiasm.

It was edging into dusk when she opened the can of creamed corn and heated her half of it in the microwave, buttered a thick slab of homemade bread—spreading it out to the edges of Herry's share as well as her own—and debated between chocolate fudge ripple and maple pecan ice cream. She wasn't allowed to share sweets with Herry, so she gave him a handful of Milk Bones.

She wouldn't get away with a meal like that if Mom were home. She didn't often get a chance to choose her own food. But she could pick anything she wanted for the next three days, until the rest of the family came home. Maybe being left behind wasn't so bad, after all.

She checked the big freezer and took out a package of lasagna to defrost for tomorrow, and hoped nobody would notice if she ate one of the pound cakes Mom kept frozen for emergency desserts.

Mandy padded barefoot through the house, hesitating before she went upstairs to go to bed. Normally nobody in Suttons Bay locked their doors. Crime was practically nonexistent, except for kids snitching candy or chips from the Market.

She looked down at Herry, ever her shadow. "You'd bark if anybody came prowling around, wouldn't you?" she asked him.

He gave his customary response, a wagging tail.

"Hmm. You never bark at anybody. And even if you did, what good would it do me if someone had already gotten inside? I guess I'll lock the doors. After all, we've never been here alone all night before."

She climbed the stairs, carrying one of her newest library books and a bowl of fresh-popped popcorn with an extra dollop of melted butter on it.

She had never felt uneasy in this house before in her life. So why did it now seem so large and so empty?

"Stupid, huh?" she asked Herry as he leaped onto the bed beside her. "It's the same house it's always been, and it was never scary before."

Maybe it was foolish to choose a spooky story to read under these circumstances. Something funny might have been more appropriate. Still, it was a mystery she'd brought upstairs, and she didn't bother to go back downstairs for a different book.

There was no one around to tell her to turn off the light and go to sleep, so she read until almost eleven o'clock.

And woke up some time later with the hair prickling all over her head, convinced she'd been awakened by some sound that shouldn't have been there.

☞ 4 ☜

Mandy lay in the darkness, all senses alert, frightened without knowing why.

Had she had a nightmare? There had been many of those since she'd been sleeping alone. But this time she didn't think she'd been dreaming anything.

She strained to remember, to recall anything that might have scared her.

A baby crying?

What a peculiar thing to be scared of, a baby crying, if that *was* what she'd heard, or dreamed, or imagined.

Of course there were no babies in the house, so it would have to be either a dream or her imagination.

Imagination had always been Mandy's friend. Imagination had filled her hours and days, had stirred her excitement, had kept her entertained. It hadn't been the same since Angel was gone, though she tried to make it work again, to take her away from the mundane world to where everything was fun and without pain.

"Herry? Did you hear anything?" she asked softly, stretching out a hand to where the big dog usually slept against her legs.

There was no dog. Again. Why did he keep leaving?

"Herry?"

Nothing.

Maybe she'd been awakened when the dog got off the bed. She was so used to having him lie against her legs. She sat up and felt the area where he was supposed to be.

It wasn't even warm. So he'd been gone for long enough for the quilt to cool off.

She was suddenly glad she'd thought to lock the doors downstairs. There was no reason to think anyone might have come into the house. She was alone, but she was perfectly safe.

Wasn't she?

Her heart refused to slow its pounding.

Had she left a radio or the TV on when she came upstairs? Had she heard something from a late-night movie? Her brothers liked horror movies, violent action movies, car chases with police sirens screaming.

Could someone have left a TV on?

In her rational mind she knew that nobody had. The boys had been gone for hours and wouldn't have left a movie running anyway. And she herself had been back and forth through the ground-floor rooms at least a dozen times since she'd been alone.

TVs didn't turn themselves on.

She couldn't hear a thing now. She never did, in the middle of the night. They were far enough from town that the sounds didn't travel from there. The road past their house led out to the deserted lighthouse, and except for a few tourists during the summer, nobody used it unless they were coming to the Sebold house.

It was calm and quiet. No storm, no wind, and there were no trees to scratch windows with skeletal branches, because the house was situated well away from the woods, out on the sand just above the beach.

If Angel had been here, they'd be making joking remarks at this point, daring each other to go downstairs and check. They'd be laughing and holding hands as they descended the stairs, and then making fun of each other when they discovered the answer was something simple like an overlooked radio that had suddenly flared to life.

Mandy didn't feel like laughing. She didn't feel like going downstairs through the darkened house, either. Not without Herry.

She called him, then, more loudly than she'd spoken before. "Herry? Where are you?"

He wasn't a watchdog. She already knew that. Herry loved everybody, friend or stranger, and the house was always full of her brothers' friends. Boys tended to eat constantly, and Herry expected them to share, everything from meat or cheese scraps to stray chips or even fruit. When the dog sat watching one of them eat, the boys would say, "Dogs don't like oranges"—or apples, or grapes, or whatever they were eating. Actually, the only thing Herry didn't eat was peas. If they put leftover stew in his dish, he carefully licked all the gravy off the peas and left them in the bottom of his bowl.

Maybe he'd gotten hungry and gone downstairs to check out his dish or to get a drink of water. Maybe the popcorn had made him thirsty.

Mandy lay still, listening. Nothing. Nothing at all.

And then, the same as the first time she had awakened, she heard the familiar click of doggy toenails on the bare wood in the hallway.

A minute later Herry crossed her darkened bedroom and leaped up beside her.

She felt a rush of relief. He'd only been hunting for Angel again.

Her arms went around his thick furry neck and she hugged him. Herry licked her cheek the way he always did.

He smelled strongly of peanut butter.

Peanut butter?

It was one of the things he loved, of course. Whenever anybody ate a peanut butter sandwich it was practically an unwritten rule: Herry got the last bite. And until they got to *his* portion, he sat watching them, drooling.

Her fingers stilled, buried in his fur. "Where did you get a peanut butter sandwich? I haven't had any since everybody left. Dogs can't open peanut butter jars."

Herry licked her again, and the smell was overpowering. There was no question but that he'd been eating peanut butter.

An idea occurred to her, causing a rush of pleasure. "Did one of the boys come home? Maybe that's what I heard."

Suddenly no longer nervous, Mandy slid out of bed. In her bare feet, with Herry gladly accompanying her, she turned on the light and headed downstairs, flicking switches as she went to illuminate her way.

It wouldn't be Gus. Nothing would distract him from playing ball. And Rude had a big weekend of tearing motorcycles apart and meeting new girls at the party on Gull Island. He wasn't likely to skip out on that.

Maybe Bert and Fairy decided that sleeping out in a tent, with no bathroom, wasn't that much fun after all. That was probably it. Fairy was having a difficult time fitting into the Sebold gang. Little things like getting sand in your shoes—or your hot dog—or drinking pop without ice in it still bothered her.

"Bert?" Mandy called out as she walked through the dining room. But there was no light in the kitchen and no response.

There was, however, an open jar of peanut butter with a knife laid across the upside-down lid, standing beside a loaf of homemade bread in a plastic bag on the kitchen table.

For a moment Mandy stood suspended in the doorway. She had *not* made herself a peanut butter sandwich. She'd eaten half a can of creamed corn with bread and butter.

"Bert?" She said her brother's name again, then crossed to the back door to check out the screened porch, in case he and Fairy had taken their snack out there to eat.

It wasn't until she'd opened the door and stepped out to find the porch deserted that she remembered. She'd locked that door, and now it was unlocked.

A walk on the beach? That wouldn't be Fairy's thing, but it might be Bert's. The entire Sebold family preferred being outside to inside the house.

She pushed open the outer screen door and called into the night. "Bert? Are you out there?"

Beside her Herry leaned against her legs, warm and

heavy. Her fingers tangled in his fur, scratching automatically behind his ears.

Dad had never felt the need to put in a yard light, but there was a floodlight at the end of the house nearest the driveway. Mandy turned it on so she could see the area where everybody parked their cars.

There were no cars. Bert and Fairy had taken off in Bert's pickup, with the tent and camping supplies in the back.

If they'd come home, the pickup would be there.

The uneasiness she'd felt when she'd awakened returned. Leaving the outside light on, she stepped back inside, flipped the hook-and-eye catch on the screened door, and stepped into the lighted kitchen. She locked that door, too.

She was positive she'd locked it before she went up to bed. If one of her brothers hadn't come home and unlocked it, who had opened it?

Bert and Fairy might have come home, she speculated, and had the truck break down before they got here, so they'd walked in from the road. That would explain the lack of a vehicle in the parking area. The first thing any of her brothers did when they walked through the door was fix something to eat.

She stared at the jar of peanut butter, the good chunky kind everybody in the family preferred.

Mom had preached it at them long enough to have

impressed the rule on each of her children: When you're finished with it, put it back where it belongs.

Nobody ever left their mess sitting on the table. Yet there it was, with the lid not even screwed back into place. A peanut butter jar. Part of a loaf of bread. A dirty knife.

Of course Mom would be gone for a couple of days. There was still time to put things away tomorrow. If they were really tired and had just wanted to go to bed, they might not have taken time to clean after themselves.

It was hard to imagine, though. Bert was trained to do it, and Fairy tried very hard not to inconvenience anyone while she was living in her in-laws' household.

"Well, *you* didn't make your own sandwich," Mandy told the dog. "So somebody's come home. It smells good, doesn't it? Guess I'll have a snack too, and then put everything away. We'll check on them when we go back upstairs."

She wound up making *two* sandwiches—one for herself and one for Herry—and wiped down the table after she'd cleared it. Herry devoured his share in two gulps and sat watching as she took the first bite of her own. "You're a pig, you know that?" she told him. "You're not getting any of mine."

Despite the declaration, she tossed him the final crust before she reached for the light switch to darken the kitchen. "Come on, let's go back to bed."

She reached for the next switch as she went through

the dining room, and then paused. There was still a faint light coming from the living room, which she hadn't noticed when coming through before because she had put on the overhead fixture in the adjoining room before she reached that doorway.

Mandy turned away from the stairs and stood on the threshold of the big room to stare at the television.

The screen was lighted, though there was no program playing. Had there been a program left on, one that included a crying child? The station was off the air now, and she couldn't remember having had the set on earlier. If her brother and his wife hadn't had time to put stuff away in the kitchen, why had they turned on the TV? she wondered rather crossly.

She crossed the room and checked to make sure there was no tape in the VCR, noting that the television was on Channel 4, the one everybody usually watched the eleven o'clock news on. She reached out and turned off the TV.

She was just beginning to feel seriously annoyed with Bert—or whichever of her brothers had come home early— when she swiveled to leave the room and saw the window.

It was standing wide open.

It had been closed when she'd been in here to pick up her library book from the shelves where all borrowed books were kept.

She was positive it had been closed because she'd

locked the front door that was right beside that window. She couldn't have helped being aware if it had stood open then, not when she was only a few feet from it. She hadn't thought to check to see if it was locked. Probably it hadn't been. They often opened windows when they wanted a breeze to move through the house, often enough so they didn't bother with locking windows in between times.

She locked it now and tested the door, to make sure *it* was still locked.

Normally she wouldn't have paid any attention to any of these things. The house was usually full of people, coming and going. It was hardly ever empty, and Mandy never thought of herself as responsible for security or anything else except her own room.

Awareness of being completely alone here now suddenly sent a prickle down her spine. "I wish you were a watchdog, Herry," she said, half under her breath. "That I could count on you to let me know if something funny's going on. If a burglar got in here, I think you'd help him carry out whatever he wanted to his waiting truck instead of barking enough to wake up everybody in the house."

Which was, she thought, only herself at the moment.

Herry's thick black tail swung gently in response to her voice.

Mandy moved to check the other windows. None of

them were locked. So much for her care with doors. She secured them all and finally headed upstairs.

In the upper hall she left the light on, and after a moment's hesitation during which she felt rather foolish, she started checking bedrooms.

Mom and Dad's. Neat, orderly, nothing out of place.

The door was closed on Bert and Fairy's room, and after a minor debate about disturbing them if they were already asleep, she knocked, then knocked louder and called out. "Bert? Fairy? Are you here?"

There was no reply, and she turned the knob, peering in.

Light spilled across the bed, disclosing no one. Not Bert and Fairy, then.

Uneasiness increasing, she went on down the hallway, opening doors on either side.

There was no sign in any one of them that their occupants had returned.

It didn't make sense.

Who had fixed sandwiches in the kitchen? Who had turned on the TV? Who had opened a window, and unlocked the back door and left it that way?

"Whoever it was," Mandy said to the dog, "they must have given you the peanut butter sandwich. You must know who it was, Herry."

But Herry wasn't talking.

What would it take for Herry to consider an intruder

to be hostile? If some thief attacked her, would Herry be protective? It didn't seem likely that a stranger would have fed the dog. Made him his own sandwich.

She'd always thought she enjoyed mysteries—in books or on TV or in made-up tales of her own—but at the moment she wasn't enjoying this one.

When Bert and Fairy got married, they'd hunted up a key for their room. So they would have privacy, Bert said. He didn't want any of his brothers walking in unannounced when Fairy was changing clothes or something.

Mandy didn't think there was another door in the house, except the outside ones, that could be locked. Certainly her own door had never had a key that she knew of.

Herry had already jumped up on the bed and was turning around to position himself in the exact right spot.

Mandy hesitated, then got the chair from her desk. She dragged it across the room and propped it under the doorknob. That's what they did in the movies. Did it really work, to keep someone from breaking in?

Not that there was any reason to think anyone would do that. She'd been all through the house, and found no trace of anyone who didn't belong there. Only indications that someone had *been* there.

Still, she felt a little better with the chair against the

door. At the very least, if anyone tried to get in, she would hear them.

For all the good that would do. She had no weapon. She wouldn't have known what to do with one if it was available.

She wished she could remember the name of the hotel where her parents were staying in Traverse City. They'd talked about several different ones, but she couldn't remember the name of any of them, let alone which one they'd settled on.

If Mom and Dad had known she would be here alone they'd have left a number where they could be reached. But they believed she was with one of her brothers, who had the number. They thought Herry was the only one still at home.

She decided to leave the light on the desk burning instead of retreating into darkness. She slid back into bed, shoving against Herry's heavy body, which was invading her space.

It wasn't until she'd pulled the quilt up over her that she realized she hadn't checked on Uncle Frank's room downstairs.

Maybe Uncle Frank had decided he didn't want to stay at Aunt Eileen's house. Maybe *he* was the one who had come home. Maybe he'd eaten a snack and gone to bed in his room downstairs. He would have known to give Herry at least part of a sandwich.

Momentarily Mandy considered going downstairs to check. She'd feel a lot better if Uncle Frank were sound asleep, with or without his meds.

If her twin had been there, they would have scampered down the stairs, giggling to find out. But somehow she couldn't quite get up the courage to do it alone. For a few seconds she quavered, imagining the rest of her life without enough courage to do anything at all. It had never been a problem when Angel was there.

She would just have to pretend, and convince herself that Uncle Frank was there, and that she was not alone with only a silly non-watchdog in this big, dark house.

Thank heaven none of the others had opted to take Herry with them when they left for this long holiday weekend.

Because then Mandy would have been truly alone, and even more scared than she was now.

She clung to Herry, convinced that there was someone in the house with her, someone who hid in the shadows and tried to be quiet, but left small traces and clues of his presence. Someone who was not a member of her own family.

Someone who was frightening her very badly.

⮞ 5 ⮜

Her dreams were disturbing.

She dreamed that she kept waking to find Herry beside her, smelling of peanut butter. She dreamed she heard someone climbing the stairs. She dreamed, again, that she heard a baby crying. She dreamed she went downstairs to check the TV, which had mysteriously turned itself back on, and once more found the window open in the living room.

When she woke up, she had trouble figuring out whether she had dreamed unfamiliar sounds or had actually heard them.

Herry apparently heard nothing, though when she woke and sat up, listening intently with her heart hammering, he raised his head and licked at her cheek.

Finally, in sheer exhaustion, Mandy slept soundly, waking to bright sunshine pouring through her window.

The desk chair was still propped under the doorknob. She looked at it, feeling rather foolish. Nobody had tried to get into her room.

She got up and went to look out the window, toward the bay. The sandy beach was clean and empty. Far out across the water a small pleasure craft left a wake that would eventually make ripples on the shore.

Normal. Everything was perfectly normal.

She pulled on jeans and a T-shirt, replaced the chair at the desk, and walked along the upstairs hall, peering through open doorways to be sure no one else had come home.

Downstairs—the living room window still closed, the TV still turned off—and through to the kitchen. Nothing out of place there, either.

Uncle Frank's room was at the end of *that* hall, on the corner facing the road, which could not be seen because of the trees. The door stood open, revealing a vacant room.

Uncle Frank had not come home. She was still by herself except for Herry.

In the daylight, there was nothing scary about the house. Mandy looked at the telephone and wondered if she should try to run down the numbers where members of her family could be contacted. But what would she say? Nothing peculiar was going on now. She'd look stupid calling for help.

Herry was nosing about in his dish, which was clearly empty.

"Okay," Mandy said, and put a scoop of dry dog food into it. Herry smelled it, then backed off, tail wagging, suggesting that she might come up with something more interesting.

She decided to have cornflakes and opened the cupboard door, but there were no cornflakes on the eye-level shelf.

"There have to be cornflakes," she said aloud. "Mom just bought two big boxes, the day before she left."

There were Cheerios, and Dad's Grape-Nuts, and Mom's Raisin Bran. Mandy stared at them, trying to figure out why they looked wrong, somehow. "Mom got two big boxes of everything, I helped put them away, so I know she did. So why is there only a single box of the Cheerios and no cornflakes?"

Herry didn't care what she fed him, as long as it wasn't dog food.

"Let's have Raisin Bran," Mandy decided. "Shall we have bananas on it?"

But the bowl on the counter, which should have had a couple of bananas left—Mom hadn't bought any more of those, thinking there would be no one home to eat them over the weekend—was empty.

If you left fruit in a bowl on a table low enough for Herry to reach it, such as the coffee table, he would help himself. Grapes, apples, peaches—he liked any of them. Oranges were safe unless they were peeled. He could even crack walnuts and carry them onto his rug in a corner of the kitchen—he was scolded for making the mess any-where else in the house—and get the meats out, leaving the shells.

He knew better than to get anything off the kitchen or dining room table or off the counters, though. Bananas, too, had to be peeled to interest him.

"I was sure there were two ripe bananas there yester-day." Mandy scowled, then gave up, fixed two heaping bowls of Raisin Bran, and opened the refrigerator for the milk.

Again, Mom hadn't stocked up on milk because every-body was going away for three days, but there had been at least a quart left in the gallon jug. Except that there was no longer a jug, only an empty space on the shelf.

"Somebody was here last night," she told Herry in dis-gust. "Somebody who pigged out on everything. Who came home and ate and then left?"

She gave up on cereal and milk, opened a can of peaches for herself, and then a can of tuna fish to dump over the dry dog food. There were still a few cookies in the jar, and she took a handful of those. She resisted the appeal in Herry's eyes until the last bite of each one, because he really wasn't supposed to have sweets. She hoped such a few tiny tastes wouldn't hurt him.

"Where do you want to walk?" she asked him. "To town? Out the beach to the lighthouse? Or out onto the road? Let's go out onto the road."

She had a sneaking suspicion that some people would consider talking to a dog the same as talking to herself. But she'd been talking to Herry all her life, and she was sure it would break his heart if she stopped. And you didn't have to be schizophrenic to speak your thoughts aloud; Mom had said so. It wasn't as if talking to a dog was the same as conversations with a tomato.

It was a quarter of a mile from the house to the road, which was blacktop, so it didn't show any tracks. Already, this early in the morning, it had warmed under the sun.

"Going to be hot this afternoon," she observed. "Maybe we'll have a few more days of swimming weather."

The nice thing about Herry was that he agreed with everything she said. Even Angel hadn't been that agreeable. His gently waving tail indicated he'd swim with her if she wanted him to.

When her sister had been alive, they'd had blanket

permission to swim whenever they liked. There was a rule, though. They weren't supposed to swim alone.

"I'm not alone," Mandy said, digging her fingers into Herry's thick coat. "You're with me, right?"

She knew perfectly well that her parents would not consider Herry the companion-for-safety they had meant. But who else was there to swim with? None of her brothers were interested any more, the way they'd been when they were younger. Not unless they had a bunch of other kids their own ages. They were keen on girls for company, but not sisters.

The road curved gently, following the sweep of the beach even though it was some distance behind her. Pines and occasional birch trees pressed close to the pavement, and a stand of sumac promised a change of color before long, when the temperatures began to drop. There was nothing else to be seen in either direction, but Herry, following some trail only his nose could detect, had turned toward the lighthouse.

"Okay," Mandy agreed. "We'll go that way." She followed behind the dog, trying to think up some kind of story she could act out to entertain herself, but nothing came to her. When she and Angel were together, they'd hardly ever failed to come up with something exciting.

Nothing was fun without Angel.

School would be starting next week. Mandy dreaded

going alone. Mom said she'd have to make some new friends this year. Everybody there would be kids she'd gone to school with since kindergarten, and to Sunday school before that.

But there wasn't anybody she could think of to try to be friends with. Everybody already had a buddy or two. Would anyone welcome her into their circle?

It would help if any of them lived out this side of town, so she could walk to school with them. There weren't any houses until you got right to the edge of Suttons Bay, and the kids there were either preschoolers or high school kids.

Ahead of her Herry had paused, sniffing the ground industriously as if he'd made a fascinating find. Herry's idea of intriguing was often something like a dead fish or a roadkill squirrel—the more powerful the odor the better. They were too far from the bay for it to be a fish, and she didn't see what he'd found when he suddenly gulped it down.

"What disgusting thing did you just eat?" Mandy demanded.

Herry licked at the road, then moved off the pavement into the trees. "If it makes you sick, it'll be your own fault," she told him. "What are you finding?"

And then she realized that the grass had been crushed down, leaving a trail into the woods. "Somebody drove off the road here. Yikes, they scraped the bark off that birch tree and—"

Her voice trailed off. Herry was already trotting into the woods, and automatically Mandy followed the trail that was all too plain. Someone had driven a car through here where there was no road, crushing grass and shrubs, nicking trees, tearing a few limbs off a young pine.

And there it was. It had come to rest squarely against a sturdy evergreen and was half buried in its spreading branches. A dark green SUV, listing to one side—a flat tire might explain its plunge off the roadway—and as Mandy came closer to it she saw that the windshield had shattered. The passenger-side door hung open, and Herry poked his nose in the car, sniffing.

Mandy made it to his side. "Somebody had a wreck," she said. "The tire's flat and the front end is caved in so they had to abandon the car. Where did they go?"

The obvious answer sprang to her mind at once. "To our house? Did they break into our house to get something to eat?"

Herry was nosing farther into the abandoned car, licking at a candy wrapper that couldn't have had anything in it but a tempting odor.

"Did they knock? Did they try to see if anybody was home? I never heard anybody knock. Were they down there prowling around in the kitchen—even turning on the TV?—while I was being scared to death?"

She hadn't checked to see if anything but food had been taken. If somebody was actually hungry, she knew her folks would have fed them. Had they used the phone to call for help, for someone to come get them? They'd had a window open, probably meaning they'd come in that way, and then it had been easier to go back out through the screened porch, and they'd left the doors unlocked that way.

Were they anyone to be afraid of? Mandy chewed briefly on her lip, considering. It wasn't very nice of them to break into a house and help themselves to groceries, but there were plenty of things around they could have stolen, and they hadn't taken toasters or radios or the TV or VCR, and the Sebolds didn't own any silver, or have much cash lying around.

She pulled her head out of the car and inspected the bad tire. It wasn't just flat, it had been blown and torn wide open. That could have been what sent them off the road.

Had they been frightened? Hurt? Unfamiliar enough with the area so they didn't know where to go, how to find help? Had they done this in the middle of the night—it was at least after dark—and if so, had they had a flashlight to find their way back to the road or to the Sebold house? And where had they gone after that?

She wished Mom and Dad were home. They always

knew what to do in an emergency. Even one of her brothers would probably have been helpful.

Where could they have been going, late at night? The road only led past Mrs. Hodge's deserted cottage and then to the lighthouse, which had been abandoned before Mandy was even born.

The cottage, then? Had the person in the car found his or her way to the little beach house, realized nobody was living there and hadn't left any provisions, then headed back toward town and stumbled on her own house?

She wasn't sure if that made her more or less nervous. She didn't know anything about this person, except that he'd had to walk away from a car that could no longer be driven. There was probably no reason to think he was dangerous, though. Was there?

"Where'd he go from here, Herry? Which direction did he take?"

Herry's tail signified his acknowledgment of her words, but no answer. Angel had been a more satisfactory companion. She was *always* a wonderful partner, never at a loss for an idea or the courage to carry through on even the wildest plan.

Mandy looked through the woods, trying to see any signs that whoever had been in the car had passed that way. She was torn between curiosity and indignation that whoever had invaded her home had almost certainly come from this damaged vehicle—and nervousness about confronting them. How could she be sure whether or not they'd be hostile or dangerous?

In an earlier time she'd have waited for her sister to decide what to do. But she knew, didn't she? Angel would have been all for following whatever trail there was and demanding answers when she found the culprits.

Angel was never again going to be there to come up with ideas and make the decisions.

Mandy swallowed. Okay, try to think like her sister.

"Did they leave a trail of scent through the woods?" she asked Herry. "Can you follow them?"

The driver, having to leave his car behind, would either have gone back to the road and returned to town, or headed through the trees to the beach. Herry was already trotting ahead of her, angling toward the bay.

Her heart began to beat a little faster at the thought of meeting the stranger face to face. He was just someone who'd had an accident, and probably thinking the house was empty, had broken in to get something to eat.

Angel wouldn't be afraid of him.

She could hear her sister's laughing voice. *"Come on. Let's go find him. We've got Herry to protect us."*

Mandy answered the unspoken words aloud. "Herry couldn't protect us from a scared cat."

"But he's big and fierce and looks like a bear, so a stranger wouldn't know that."

Herry was already well ahead of her, coming out of the trees onto the beach. Mandy drew a deep breath and followed him. She knew Angel so well she could correctly come up with whatever her sister would think or say or do. All she had to do, then, was pretend that Angel was with her, and she'd be fine.

Stepping out of the shadowed woods, soaked in the fragrance of sun-warmed pines, Mandy saw that she'd emerged right alongside Mrs. Hodge's forlorn little cottage. Herry kept on going, headed for the bay, lapping up a drink.

Mandy was immediately aware that the broom that had been left leaning against the dock the day before was gone, and her heartbeat quickened as she waited for her sister's comment on *that*.

≈ 6 ≈

Somebody had moved the broom.

Who?

Mandy walked across the sand toward her dog, notic-ing that he'd left bearlike footprints at the edge of the lap-ping waves. He was right where the little print had been yesterday, but the moving water wiped out that one.

Had the person driving the car had a little kid with him? Or her?

Overhead a seagull soared, its cry a familiar sound. There was nothing else moving in either direction.

Herry had finished drinking and was again sniffing with his nose to the ground. Following a scent? Mandy tried to make out tracks, but the loose sand, far from smooth, wouldn't hold a footprint.

Herry stopped, looking back at her for guidance. Which way did she want to go?

Normally she walked past the small cottage without noticing it. Today Mandy decided to check it out.

Up close, it was even shabbier than she'd remembered. The paint had been weathered to the point that you couldn't tell it had ever looked like anything but driftwood. The broom stood leaning against the wall near the side door.

Automatically Mandy tried the knob, which resisted her efforts. She shaded her eyes to peer into a kitchen window, which hadn't been washed in a very long time, but she couldn't see much of anything.

Stubbornly, she moved along the wall, trying a different window. The first two had curtains drawn over them, so she went around the corner to the side away from the beach.

An old galvanized washtub had been placed under the window there, as if someone had stood on it to make it easier to climb in the window.

Mandy stepped onto it and reached upward to test the window. It slid open under her hands.

See if anybody's in there.

It was almost as if her sister were standing behind her, making the suggestion. Being with Angel had always given her the courage to do things she'd never have done on her own. Angel had seldom been afraid of anything.

Mandy didn't know for sure if she was afraid now or not. What would she do if she climbed in the window and encountered strangers? Trespassers, because if they belonged in there they'd have had a key and gone through a door.

Herry had followed her and stood patiently, waiting for whatever she was going to do.

She couldn't lift him up to go inside, he weighed more than she did. Still, it made her feel better to know he was there, an indication to anyone looking for her that she was in the vicinity.

Not that anyone would look for her before Monday night, when her family came home.

Go on, go in. It's just a deserted cottage. Nobody'll care one way or the other if you go in.

Unless, of course, the people who had fled the wrecked car were in there.

Mandy stuck her head through the opening and looked inside. She saw a bedroom—with a bed stripped down to the mattress—across the room, and a wooden dresser just below the window, handy for stepping onto.

"Hello! Is anybody here?" she called out.

There was no response.

Unexpectedly, Herry nudged her leg and almost made her fall off the washtub. She grabbed for the window ledge to keep her footing.

"Cut it out! I'm thinking!" she told him. She wondered if he'd continue to stand there, bushy tail gently waving, if she'd been jerked inside by unseen hands and disappeared from sight.

The smart thing was probably just to go home, lock herself inside her own house, and get on the phone and try to locate some member of her family.

Or she could walk into town and find the town cop. There was a tiny police station, manned by one of three men, right next door to the post office. They had two police cars, which they shared, and there was no telling exactly where the man on duty might be at any specific time.

The worst crime they ever had to deal with was when kids played some prank on Halloween or swiped something from the market or the hardware store. Mostly Dad dealt with young thieves on his own if he spotted them. He knew every kid in town and wouldn't bother with police at all. Unlike the way things were done these days in the cities, in Suttons Bay, if he told their parents, justice was swiftly administered without denying the culpability of their offspring.

She should report the wrecked car, but she didn't want to tell a cop the rest. What would she say? Somebody broke into our house in the middle of the night and made a snack. They didn't take as much food as Mom would have given them if she'd been home. They didn't steal anything else, as far as she could tell, and certainly hadn't threatened her.

Mandy couldn't imagine herself going to the police station. Angel, yes, but not her.

Herry was looking up at her, and Mandy made up her mind. She swung a leg over the sill and lowered herself onto the dresser, then jumped onto the floor.

She'd been in Mrs. Hodge's home before the old lady took sick. It had only one bedroom, a kitchen, and a tiny living room. It had a bathroom the size of a closet, with no tub. Mrs. Hodge had bathed in the washtub, the way the pioneers used to do.

Mandy walked through the rooms, which were reasonably tidy except for dust, and there wasn't even much of that. Sand didn't translate into dust, just a drifting of pale grains that had blown in around a kitchen window.

The furniture, all of it old and worn, had been left behind when personal belongings had been removed.

But something new had been added very recently.

On the checked plastic tablecloth on the kitchen table stood the remains of a gallon jug of milk and the boxes of cereal missing from the Sebold house. Plus the opened container of Uncle Frank's graham crackers that she hadn't noticed was missing.

Part of the mystery solved.

There was no one here now. There was nowhere to hide, if they'd heard her coming. Just tiny, empty rooms with the door standing open to the only closet, where a few hangers remained. *No reason to think that somebody who'd wrecked their car and borrowed some food would be dangerous.*

Maybe now, in daylight, they'd walked back to town for help.

Moments later, Mandy climbed up on the dresser and went out the same way she'd come in.

Herry had settled into a comfortable position with his head resting on his paws. He stood up as soon as Mandy was ready to go.

"If only you could talk," she told him. "You could tell me who made you the sandwich last night."

He recognized the word "sandwich." Her brothers had taught him a lot of key words, much to Mom's annoyance, because now whenever anyone used any of them, he got excited. At least as excited as Herry ever got. That meant getting to his feet, wagging his tail, and if food was involved, drooling until it was provided for him.

"I'm sure glad you stayed home with me," Mandy told him now. "Let's go home and see if I can figure out how to get in touch with somebody. Just in case I need to."

Maybe she could add imagination to the reality and make up a story. She'd tried before, but without her sister to play one of the parts, and Herry willing but unable to talk, it hadn't been successful. How was she ever again going to come up with anything that was fun?

She tried. What if the car crashed in the woods had had somebody wounded still in it? Covered with blood where they'd hit their head on that cracked windshield? Or what if the driver had had a bullet hole in his head? She'd have run home, breathless, to call the police.

Okay, call a deputy, who would possibly come with lights and sirens, and everybody in town trailing along behind to see what was happening. Or would a cop have come quietly, if she told him the victim was already dead?

She didn't want to touch anybody to check their pulse. But if the bullet hole was in their head, she could be pretty sure the guy was dead.

Who would have shot him? How would they have done it while he was driving? Had the killer been in the car with him?

A killer who liked graham crackers.

Well, if you were making up stuff, you just kept the parts that were useful. And no doubt some murderers *did* eat graham crackers.

When the twins were in fifth grade they'd had an author come to speak to their class. He told them one of the ways he thought up stories to write was to play "What if?" Take a real situation and speculate on what might develop that hadn't really happened, but *might* have.

The twins had made up a number of thrillers based on "What if?" So far her scenario sounded like something her sister would have come up with. And Mandy herself would have been the one pointing out the flaws in it.

When they were little, the twins had both liked paper dolls. Angel usually wound up with her people flying through the air, while Mandy preferred something more ordinary. Especially when Angel tore up the fragile dolls when they crashed into each other.

Mandy had usually chosen story ideas that were more realistic than flying people. At least dealing with things that were *feasible*.

But there was no rule that said an idea had to be realistic. It could be science fiction, complete with aliens, if she wanted it to be.

On the other hand, Mandy had never had that kind of imagination. She liked things that were possible, even if they weren't very likely.

Having someone break into your house for snacks, or wrecking a car in the woods, were not likely, but they'd happened.

She thought about it, walking home with Herry brushing against her hand. What if the driver of the car was a fugitive? From where? From what? There were no prisons nearby, nothing she could think of that the driver had been running away from if he'd escaped from jail.

She reached home and started up the back steps. And stopped, her heart suddenly racing once more.

Someone had kicked over one of the pots of dirt that had been sitting on the end of the bottom step waiting for Mom to plant whatever she brought home from the nursery in Traverse City on Monday. That was going to be her anniversary present to herself. Not much of anything except pine tree, chokecherries, and sumac grew in the sand, so Mom kept a few flowers and ivylike plants in pots inside the house.

Mandy hadn't even noticed the pot when she left the house. And Herry would not have knocked it over. Herry was unerringly careful about where he put his feet. His only failing in that regard was his refusal to attempt to climb a ladder, like the one at the lighthouse.

Now the pot of dirt had spilled onto the step, and right in the middle of the dirt was a footprint, leading into the house.

7

In the past Mandy and her sister had often seemed to read one another's minds. They could almost always exchange a glance and know immediately what the other was thinking. They hadn't necessarily had to speak the words to plan a prank to play on their brothers or their teachers.

And just that morning Mandy had created courage in herself by her conviction of what Angel would have said or thought or done.

She stared at the footprint.

Herry paused behind her, waiting for her to decide whether to go in the house or not.

She could go in and confront whoever was in there. She had no doubt it was the same person who had wrecked the car in the woods and stolen food from the kitchen and apparently taken refuge in the cottage down the beach.

What would Angel do?

She spoke the answer to the dog just behind her. "She'd march in and tell them to put their hands up. Even if she didn't have a gun."

If Angel did it, the intruder would probably reach for the ceiling. Mandy's confidence wavered.

She didn't have to go into the house. She could head for town and call the deputy and ask him to investigate.

Angel would never ask a deputy for help.

"Who am I? Me, or Angel? Would the things she'd have done work for me, too?"

Herry made no reply.

"If you can't do anything about your situation," Mom would say, "change your attitude. It's the only thing you can control."

Except, of course, that if she stiffened her spine and changed her attitude to confidence instead of apprehension, she could be in real trouble if she encountered an invader with a hostile mind-set.

This wasn't a little kid. She looked at the shoe print. *About a size ten,* she thought. The same as Gus's. Gus was fifteen.

She'd occasionally been able to wrestle Gus to the

ground, if she surprised him and tickled him. Of course he probably hadn't fought as hard as if she had been one of the brothers. She couldn't count on an intruder/thief holding back because she was a girl.

"Maybe he'd be intimidated by a huge dog that looks like a bear," she muttered, before she remembered that whoever he was, he'd made Herry a sandwich. Not likely he'd be afraid of the dog now.

Herry, tired of waiting for her to move, nudged the back of her leg.

She was still trying to decide what to do when she heard a car turning into the driveway.

Relief washed over her. Somebody was coming home, and she had backup.

Only it wasn't Mom and Dad, or any of her brothers. The car was older than anything the Sebolds owned, except for Bert's Ford pickup. There was a dent in the left front fender, but it was otherwise well maintained, an older black van with dark windows. Not many people in this part of the country drove cars with windows you couldn't see through.

Not family.

All her life Mandy had loved living where they did, right on the beach with a strip of woods between the house and the road, several miles from town, in wonderful isolation. It was private and quiet.

Except for the noisy engine, it was silent now, and the lack of neighbors within shouting distance made her nervous.

The man at the wheel leaned out of his open window and called to her. "Hi! You live here?"

"Yes," Mandy said uncertainly. She'd had all the don't-talk-to-strangers warnings. Were they more or less valid when the strangers drove into your own yard?

"We'd like to ask you a couple of questions," he said. The man in the passenger seat was ducking his head slightly so that he, too, could look at Mandy.

She made no response to that, wondering if the intruder in the house was aware that a car had driven almost up to the steps.

"We're looking for a young fellow in a dark green SUV."

Mandy's heart rate quickened instantly, and her tongue went more or less numb.

"You seen anybody like that?"

Possible replies flickered through her mind. *He's probably in my kitchen right now, stealing some more food. Or if he went out a window on the other side of the house, he could be hiding in Mrs. Hodge's cottage by this time.*

She decided on a simple and truthful "No."

She shifted position so that their view of the footprint was blocked.

"You sure? Young guy, skinny, driving an Explorer?"

A scowl began to form creases on her forehead. Why did the man persist in questioning what she had just told him? "I haven't seen anyone like that." She didn't say she hadn't seen the car, and she wasn't sure why she wasn't frank about mentioning the stranger they were undoubtedly looking for.

The driver was fairly young, probably in his thirties, wearing a suit and tie. Not many people around Suttons Bay, other than Pastor Swenhold, wore a suit and tie except at church. He smiled. "Maybe I could talk to your mother or dad? See if they've seen the boy or the Explorer?"

She had been told never to admit to anyone, even on the phone, that she was home alone. Actually, that was seldom the case, and though she made up lots of stories, she wasn't used to lying.

"There's no one here but us kids," she settled for. The memory of her sister, who was still strongly here in her mind, and Herry, who thought he was their little brother—that didn't make it a lie, did it?

"Maybe you could ask them? Make sure?" The smile on the man's face was fixed.

"No, I don't think so. Nobody saw any such person." Belatedly, she realized that Herry had seen the intruder, which made it an inadvertent lie, but she didn't correct it.

"Can you tell me when your parents will be home?"

She avoided saying something unwise by shrugging her shoulders. She put down a hand and took hold of Herry's collar, hoping the man would think she was holding him back so he wouldn't attack. Or that it would be smart to stay in his car for fear that he *would*.

The man reached into an inner pocket and pulled out a business card, extending it toward her. "When they do, would you ask them to call this number? They may have seen something you didn't notice."

Mandy didn't move. She didn't want to walk out to the car and accept the card. She didn't know if it was because she was home alone or because there was something suspicious about the men—after all, nothing like this had ever happened before—but instinct held her on the porch steps.

Angel, what shall I say to him? she wondered.

And the words came. "Why are you looking for him?"

"It's important that we talk to him," the man said, which was hardly an answer.

"I'm not supposed to talk to strangers," she said finally when the man's smile was beginning to look somewhat strained. "I have to go now."

She turned in a way to smudge the footprint in the spilled dirt, and, pulling Herry with her to suggest he had to be controlled, she opened the screened door and went onto the porch.

Right this minute the hungry intruder who might be inside seemed less risky than the two men in the car.

"Hey, wait!" The stranger called after her, but she pretended not to hear.

The door was standing open between the porch and the kitchen. She closed it behind her and locked it before she turned to look out at the car.

It remained where it had stopped, the driver now glaring toward the house. He turned to say something to his companion, and she wished she could hear what it was.

She watched the van door open and the driver get out. Mandy stepped back from the window and crouched beside Herry, her heart racing. Would the man try to force open the door? What about the window or the back door?

She considered running out the back, but the footsteps were already coming across the porch. The man didn't knock or try to open the door. Mandy heard the footsteps leave again, followed by the slam of the van door and the sound of the vehicle leaving. She let her breath out and stood up.

She'd almost forgotten the intruder with the size ten shoe. She looked around now and saw a cupboard door standing ajar, proving he'd been here again.

"If he's here, Herry, go find him," she suggested. Herry gently wagged his tail, watching her hands. They were in the kitchen, after all, and that should mean that food would be forthcoming.

She didn't bother to find a dog biscuit. "Well, the least you can do is come with me while I make sure he's gone," she said crossly.

He was quite willing to do that. He trailed her into the dining room—nothing out of place there—and into the living room, where it was as she'd left it. She found the open window in Uncle Frank's room.

Her uninvited guest had heard the car, heard her voice, and bailed out in too much of a hurry to close it behind him.

Why were the men chasing him?

Had he stolen the car?

It suddenly occurred to her that there was probably identification, indicating ownership of the car at least, in the glove compartment. She ought to go back and see.

As she was leaving the room, she noticed the small prescription container on Uncle Frank's desk. He'd gone off without his medication. She hoped Aunt Eileen would keep him away from the market and any other public place where his behavior would cause trouble.

Had he deliberately left it behind? More than likely. Maybe if he talked to tomatoes or did something else bizarre, Aunt Eileen would bring him back home to get the medication. Maybe she should call her, just to make her aware that Uncle Frank was off his pills, and then casually mention her visitors and the invasion of their kitchen.

Since they were now walking toward the kitchen again, Herry moved ahead of her, and she nearly tripped over him.

Herry endured being stepped on with great patience. Most of the time he didn't even yip. Mandy made her way around him to the kitchen phone and dialed her aunt's number.

It rang five times before it was answered.

A male voice. "Yeah?"

"Uncle Frank? It's Mandy. May I speak to Aunt Eileen?"

"Not here," Frank said.

"She left you alone?"

"Me and the dog. We're having corn on the cob for supper. And fresh fish."

"Good. Will you ask her to call me when she comes home? There's something I need to talk to her about."

"She's busy," the old man asserted, and Mandy spoke quickly before he could hang up.

"There's something peculiar going on and I need to talk to a grown-up. There's a wrecked car in the woods, and somebody broke into the house and took food. And then a couple of men came in a car and asked questions. I don't know what I should do."

"Okay. I'll tell her," Frank said.

"Do you know you left your medicine here? Maybe she should come over and get it."

"I don't like it. I don't want it. I don't need it."

"Didn't you promise Mom you'd take it? So people wouldn't complain about you?"

"That wasn't really Beatrice," Frank told her. "There's a woman who hides behind her mask. She doesn't like me."

"No, it was really Mom. And you agreed to take the pills."

"How do I know you're the real Mandy?"

"It's really me, Uncle Frank. Remember how we made the toasted cheese sandwiches when we were by ourselves last week, and we finished off the cherry ice cream?"

"Somebody could have told you about that. I have to go let the dog out."

"Have Aunt Eileen call me, okay?" she said quickly, and stood there after he'd hung up, wondering if he'd remember or if, convinced that she was another imposter, he would fail to deliver the message.

The black van was gone from the yard when she looked out. She wondered why the man had come up to the door but hadn't knocked. She looked out at the driveway; the van had not returned. Cautiously, Mandy opened the door and saw something white flutter to the doormat.

It was an ordinary business card, with no useful information printed on it. She read it aloud. "Kirby L. Mason, Attorney-at-Law." There was a phone number that she recognized by the area code as being in southern Michigan, but he had crossed off that number and written another one beneath it. She thought that area code was in Traverse City. There was no street address.

Having a business card didn't mean the man had been here on a legitimate errand. Anybody with a computer could make up a business card saying anything they wanted.

She stuck it in the pocket of her jeans to show to her parents or Aunt Eileen, whichever of them showed up first.

"Let's go look in the glove compartment of that car," she said to Herry, and he fell into place beside her.

They cut through the woods, not risking going out onto the road where Mr. Mason might still be looking for the driver of the SUV. Had he driven on past the Sebold driveway, so that he might notice where the car had swerved off into the woods, or had he turned back because of the sign that advised the road was not maintained past that point?

She wasn't sure why she was so much more suspicious of Kirby Mason than she was of the driver of the damaged car. Someone who'd had an accident wasn't as

intimidating as two guys asking questions without expla-
nations or answers to *her* concerns.

Sunlight filtered through the trees, making patterns
on her bare arms. Mandy loved this time of year, when
it was still warm but the leaves would be turning color
soon, and there was a lovely autumny smell in the air.
She and Angel had roamed the beach and the woods,
visiting all the old familiar places that her brothers
didn't bother with anymore. Places like the lighthouse
and the old fort Bert and Bel had built when they were
little kids, deeper into the woods on the far side of the
road, and the remains of a wigwam, made of sticks, that
Rude and Gus had constructed when they were the age
that she was now.

Far out on the point, half a mile short of the lighthouse, there were remains of the old cherry cannery,
where the bay dropped off to deep water just a few feet
from shore. The building had crumbled, the roof fallen
in, and there were only a few thick pilings remaining of
the dock, close to shore where the boats had brought in
loads of the cherries for which Michigan was famous, and
then taken out the canned product.

All of it was deserted, silent. Nonthreatening, peaceful,
and familiar. She and her twin had spent endless sum-
mers here and made up and acted out hundreds of
stories. She hadn't really thought about it until it was too

late, but she'd expected their lives to go on in the same way until they were grown up.

For a moment the pain clawed at her again, making a cramp in her chest. She was alone now. They would never go on to high school together, never play any more tricks on anyone, never graduate or have their first dates together. They had even planned who those dates would be—Dale VanAllsburg for Angel and Conrad Hall for Mandy. Both boys were far too silly now to be even worth talking to, but they were smart and fairly good looking and they were both funny.

Mom and Dad said having a sense of humor was one of the most important things to look for in a boyfriend. But Mom had said the girls couldn't date until they were at least sixteen, and in five years surely Dale and Conrad would have grown out of their immaturity.

Gone. All the dreams and plans were gone. Mandy swallowed as she spotted the dark green SUV through the trees, with the passenger side door still hanging open as she'd found it.

Herry was already sniffing around it, filling the open doorway, and she pulled him back out of her way and reached for the button to open the glove compartment.

It opened with a click and she reached for the stack of registration papers inside. As she was withdrawing to look at them, there was a sudden movement in the backseat and a head reared up with a grunt of surprise.

Mandy jerked upright, smacking her head hard on the door frame, emitting a yelp of anguish.

For a moment she saw black spots, and when they cleared, she had no doubt that she was facing the mysterious invader.

He stared at her, wild-eyed, dark hair sticking up in uncombed spikes, lower jaw sagging open.

He wasn't much older than she was.

The first thing that came into her head was, "Were you the one driving this car?"

He gulped. "Uh, yeah."

"Do you even have a license to drive?" He was smaller than she'd have expected by the size of his shoes.

He licked his lips, even more disconcerted than she was. "I—I'm sixteen," he asserted.

It was Angel's observation that came to her lips. "You look more like twelve."

His face flamed red. "Well, I *will* be sixteen."

"Maybe in two or three years." Her fears had virtually faded away. He was smaller than Gus, and she didn't know if he was ticklish, but he wasn't as sturdy as her brother. He didn't look like someone who could do her any bodily harm. "I think somebody's looking for you."

The color slid out of his face as if a plug had been pulled that drained it of blood.

"What—what do you mean?" His voice squeaked.

"Two guys in an old black van drove into our yard a little while ago. They were looking for a green SUV and a skinny kid."

His top teeth sank into his lower lip. "Did you tell them—?"

"I didn't tell them anything. Not even that you broke into my house and stole food."

"I—I'm sorry, but we were hungry and I didn't think anybody was home or would miss it—"

"Did you steal the car? Does it belong to them?" Her confidence grew by the moment. He didn't look any more dangerous than any of the boys who would be in her sixth grade class when school started.

"No. I mean, it doesn't belong to *them*. And I didn't steal it, exactly."

"What does that mean? Exactly? Either you stole it or you didn't." Angel again.

He moistened his lips again. "It's a long story."

"Are you hiding from those men?"

"I'm trying to. Look, I *do* need help. Just for a few days."

"Why don't you call the police if they're threatening you?" Already her mind was spinning, coming up with story ideas for what might be his answers.

"I can't," he said quickly. "They'd never believe me. My dad will believe me, but he's in Japan right now. I have to hide until he comes back."

"Why won't the police believe you? If you just tell them the truth—"

"They'll lie. Kirby and Larry will lie." He leaned toward her, resting his arms on the back of the front seat, his expression earnest. "Look, if you'd just help me hide— and give me something to eat, for a couple of days—"

There was pleading in his dark eyes now, at least the beginning of hope.

Mandy spoke as if she were writing a story. "I think you better tell me what's going on. What's happened."

He sucked in a breath that made his chest rise and fall. "It—it's kind of hard to believe."

"Try me. What did you do to make those men chase you?"

His gaze skittered back and forth before resettling on hers. "It sounds worse than it is."

"What'll they do to you if they find you? Turn you over to the police?"

He gave a sort of laugh, though it was clearly from nervousness, not amusement. "Oh, no! The last thing they'd do would be to turn me over to the cops!"

Mandy sensed that he was far more scared than she had been, and her own fear of him was rapidly evaporating.

"Did you kill somebody?" Mandy asked, the worst thing she could imagine.

Now he was chewing on his bottom lip, and the expression that came over his face reminded Mandy of her brother Gus when he was trying to decide which lie to tell. "Umm, it's hard to explain. You're probably not going to believe it."

She was still rubbing gingerly at her head, where a lump was rising. "Maybe if you just told the truth," she suggested.

He looked as if he were about to jump off a precipice, or into a fire. Then he blurted out his story. "I kidnapped my little brother," he said, and waited for her to call him a liar.

∽ 8 ∾

He didn't expect to be believed. In fact, Mandy would have decided that his claim was absurd except for one thing.

"You tried to erase his footprints from the beach in front of Mrs. Hodge's cottage."

The boy blinked. He hadn't been expecting that. "Did I miss some?"

"Beside the dock, at the edge of the water."

Mandy was beginning to feel like Alice down the rabbit hole, disoriented and confused.

"You kidnapped your little brother—after you'd stolen a car, which you aren't old enough to drive—and you wrecked it here in the woods, and then you broke into my house and stole food," she summed up, "and what have you done with your little brother?"

"Uh, he's asleep. In my great-grandmother's cottage. I was . . . I had to come back here and look for something before he wakes up."

"Your great-grandmother's cottage?"

"My great-grandmother was Oribel Hodge. I guess she doesn't live there anymore."

"If she was your great-grandmother, how come you didn't know she died? More than a year ago?"

He *had* known her name, though. Oribel was not exactly a common name.

"She was my mother's grandmother. I didn't know her very well. We visited her here once, about six years ago. After Mom died, my dad didn't stay in touch with her. They didn't like each other very much. Nobody notified our family she'd died. At least not as far as I know."

"And who are you?"

Again there was hesitancy. "I'm Zander Vyland. Short for Alexander."

Mandy had withdrawn a sheaf of papers from the glove compartment, and now she looked down at them.

"The registration says Rupert and Giselle Vyland. That's your parents?"

"My dad and my stepmother. Do you mind if I get out of here and go back to the cottage? Dusty might wake up and be scared."

"Did you find what you were looking for?"

Zander held up a leather wallet. "It fell through into the backseat. There isn't much money in it, but I'll need all there is when I dare to go to town."

He opened the back door and got out, and she saw that he was, indeed, very skinny and quite tall. Her glance dropped to his shoes. They were black-and-white athletic shoes, large for the size of the rest of him.

"I think you owe me an explanation." Not very long ago, she wouldn't have dreamed of making such a demand of a stranger. It made a difference that she wasn't afraid of him any longer. "Let's go see if your little brother is okay. Why did you kidnap him?"

Zander sighed deeply. "I had to, before *they* did."

"Who's *they*?" They started off through the woods, toward the beach and the cottage this time. Herry sniffed the papers in Mandy's hand and, finding nothing to eat, checked out the boy as well.

"Those guys in the car that came looking for me. Kirby and Larry. Sooner or later they'll find the car and know I'm here somewhere. If I can keep moving, or hide until next week, when my dad and Giselle get home from Japan, they won't be able to do anything. I don't think." That last sounded as if he were not quite sure.

"Who are they? The men in the black van?"

"Kirby and Larry. Kirby is Carol's brother."

Mandy stopped walking, staring at him in exasperation.

"Is this supposed to make sense to me? Who's *Carol*?"

"The babysitter. They wanted her to cooperate, help them, but she got scared and ran away. I think."

"I'm going to need a printed-out diagram to keep track of all this." Suspicion crept into her voice. "It's too crazy. If you're making it up, you need something that makes sense."

"I can't help it; it *is* crazy." Zander looked at her in despair, then started walking again. The bay could now be seen between the trees. "Look, I'm sorry about the stuff I stole out of your kitchen. I didn't think there was anybody home, and I only took enough to keep Dusty and me from starving. I didn't dare go into town to a store, for fear Kirby and Larry would spot me or the car—and I don't have much money, anyway. When my dad gets home, he'll pay for it. I'm sure he'll pay for it. If you can help keep me from being caught before then, he might even give you a reward." He glanced at her hopefully.

They came out of the woods on the beach and crossed toward the cottage. "We'll have to go in the window," Zander said. "The door's locked and I couldn't see any way to open it."

"I know," Mandy said. "It sounds to me like you need more help than I can give you."

"Maybe your family? If you explain to them what a mess I'm in?"

"I can't explain anything until I understand it a lot better than I do now. My family won't be back until Monday night, and I don't even know how to reach any of them, unless my aunt comes over to pick up Uncle Frank's medicine. And he doesn't want to take it, so he probably won't even tell her I called."

Zander rubbed a hand across his mouth. "And you think *I'm* incoherent."

They had reached the cottage. By unspoken consent they rounded the house to where the window stood open, and Mandy climbed through first. Resignedly, Herry lay down and rested his muzzle on his gigantic paws.

There was a little boy, maybe two years old, curled up asleep on the bare mattress in the bedroom. He'd been sucking his thumb, and it had fallen almost all the way out of his mouth. He had very fair hair, nearly white, and he was wearing a disposable diaper and a striped T-shirt.

She would certainly have been amazed if she'd found him alone when she was here earlier.

Zander came through the open window behind her and gestured that she was to go out into the main room. There was still a kitchen table there, and several chairs. They sat down on opposite sides of the table and stared at each other.

"Do you think your parents would help me?" Zander asked finally.

"When they come home, probably. If they believe your story." Mandy hesitated. "I don't think they'll approve either of your taking the car or kidnapping anybody. The trouble is, I don't know how to get hold of them to get them to come home."

Zander pushed a hand through his hair, leaving it standing in peaks. "It might be a matter of life and death."

"Are you serious?"

The boy inhaled deeply, then blew the air out of his lungs. "Oh, yeah. I don't think Larry and Kirby will dare to leave me alive if they catch up with me. I don't think they'd hurt Dusty, they want the ransom for him, and he's too little to tell anybody what they did. But he'd be really scared."

The twins had made up dozens of mysteries. Some of them had been pretty wild, with Angel wanting to bring in science-fictiony elements, and Mandy trying to stay with something more realistic. She felt as if she'd fallen into one of her sister's scripts. This didn't sound like intergalactic visitors, but it didn't sound likely, either.

Yet there was no doubting Zander Vyland's fear. And whether he'd been kidnapped or not, there was certainly a little boy sleeping in the next room. And a wrecked car out in the woods, where Zander's pursuers might well find it if they came back and continued their search on foot.

"There's no way to hide that car," Mandy mused. "I guess you can't drive it out of there."

"No. I tried."

"Okay," she said. "Start from the beginning and tell me what this is all about."

It took quite a while, with Mandy interjecting occasional questions.

Zander and Dusty, his half brother, lived with their parents, Rupert and Giselle. Mr. Vyland owned and operated a chain of department stores headquartered in Detroit. The family owned a summer home on the eastern shore of Grand Traverse Bay, opposite Northport Point. The family had been there for several weeks when something came up that required Rupert's presence in Japan.

"He's got partners there. He flies back and forth several times a year, and sometimes Mr. Soto comes to Detroit. This time Dad wanted Giselle—my stepmother—to go with him. She does, sometimes. Only Dusty had some kind of ear infection, and they couldn't take him. It would hurt his ears, the pressure on the airplane, you know?"

Mandy had never been on an airplane and had no idea how that worked, but she nodded attentively.

"So anyway, I was going to stay here with Carol, the babysitter, and they decided to leave Dusty, too. He was on antibiotics and nobody thought he was in serious condition, he just couldn't risk flying until his ears cleared up."

"They didn't ask you to go?" Mandy thought it would be fun to fly to Japan, or anywhere else.

"No, they never take me anywhere. Well, once to Miami. They've got nice beaches there, so that was okay. But they don't do anything interesting when they get where they're going. Just business meetings. Carol and Dusty and I went on the beaches in Miami, but not my dad.

"It was by accident that I heard them talking," Zander went on. "I'd gone to bed, but I got hungry about midnight and went downstairs to raid the refrigerator. Only the lights were on down there, and I heard voices. Carol and her brother Kirby, and his friend Larry." He rubbed a hand over the lower part of his face, looking exhausted. "Carol's okay, but I don't like either Kirby or Larry. They're jerks. They never came to see Carol when Dad or Giselle were home, but when my folks left, they started coming by. Then they acted as if I was invisible, and it annoyed them if Dusty cried or anything and needed Carol's attention."

So far this was sounding normal, nothing unusual. Mandy waited for him to continue.

"I didn't really care what they were talking about," Zander went on. "I just hung around for a minute to see if they'd go away. I didn't intend to go in and make a sandwich while those two goons were there. Kirby, especially, has always made it plain he doesn't like me."

"He left a business card at my house. It said he was a lawyer, but it didn't give an address for him. Just a phone number."

"Yeah, I guess he's a lawyer. A dishonest one, I think. No address because he doesn't maintain an office in one place. I think he moves so people can't find him when he's messed up their case or something. He uses a cell phone."

"So what did you hear when you were eavesdropping?"

"I wasn't—" Zander began defensively, then changed the tone of his voice. "Well, it wasn't deliberate, at least not until Carol said, '*No!* I won't do it! I love Dusty, and this is a good job, and I won't jeopardize it!'"

He swallowed hard, making his Adam's apple go up and down. "And then Kirby says in that smarmy way he talks when he's trying to con Carol into loaning him money or something, 'There's no reason why you should lose your job, sis. It won't be your fault if somebody snatches the kid.'"

Zander took another swipe at his hair, which kept falling in his face. "Well, would you have quit listening when you heard him say that? About 'snatching the kid' and Carol's shoving her chair away from the table and starting to yell? 'What family is going to keep a nanny who lets their baby get kidnapped, you idiot?' she says, and Kirby says back, 'Lower your voice, they can hear you a mile away. We can work this out so it looks like you had nothing to do with it. Why should they suspect you? You been taking care of the kid since he was born, practically. If you want we can tie you up, maybe leave a lump on your head.'"

By this time Mandy was mesmerized. It was as intriguing as one of her own wildest stories. At the same time, Zander was convincing. Not only that he was telling the truth, but that he was scared.

"Weren't you afraid they'd find out you were listening?"

"I didn't think of that until later, and then I was scared spitless. As soon as Kirby suggested a lump on her head, Carol was practically screaming. Both the guys were trying to calm her down, and her rotten brother said they'd give her a cut of the ransom money, and that made her all the madder. I couldn't see any of them, I was around the corner in the dining room, but I head a chair go over with a crash, and I could tell from the sounds that one of the guys had put his hand over her mouth to shut her up."

The boy had begun to tremble by this time. "I didn't dare stick around to hear any more, but I couldn't help getting what Kirby said about it being a great chance to do it, with my dad and Giselle out of the country, and they wouldn't know about it or call the cops until he got back. Plenty of time to get away. And Larry said, 'What about the other kid?' Meaning *me*. And Kirby said, 'He'll sleep through the whole thing. If he doesn't, we'll knock him over the head too.'" Another gulp. "About then, with me stumbling around in the near dark to get away and trying not to run into anything that would make a noise and give me away, Carol got her mouth free and yelled, 'You leave Zander alone too!' and by that time I just gave up and ran back up the stairs."

He looked at Mandy across the table, clenching and unclenching his hands until his knuckles were white.

"And I knew what I had to do," Zander said with a quaver in his voice. "I had to grab Dusty and escape. So I did."

A small whimper brought their attention toward the bedroom door as the tousled blond toddler emerged. One thumb trailed from his mouth, and his diaper sagged in a way that suggested it was full.

"Hi, Dusty," Zander said. "Come and meet—gosh, I don't even know your name." He waited for her to give it.

"Amanda Sebold. Everybody calls me Mandy."

Dusty glanced at her, then rushed across the room to bury his face in his brother's lap.

"Can you say hi to Mandy?"

Burrowing deeper into Zander's knees, Dusty shook his head.

"He smells," Mandy observed.

"Yeah. I'll change him." Zander stood up and led his

little brother to the ratty old couch that hadn't been worth removing when they cleared out the cottage. He swung Dusty onto it and reached for the blue diaper bag.

He'd obviously changed diapers before. He wadded up the dirty one and stuck it in a plastic bag. "I don't know what to do with these. If I leave them around anywhere and Kirby and Larry find them, they'll know which way we went."

"If they drive past our driveway, beyond the 'Road Not Maintained' sign, they'll see where your car went off the road. So they'll know where you left it."

"What's at the end of the road?"

"No more houses beyond this one. The falling-down remains of the cherry cannery are still there, half a mile down, no roof and you could fall through the floor, it's so rotten. There's a lighthouse on the point, boarded up, 'Keep Out' signs on it. We pulled off a board and got inside, but it's empty on the ground floor, and it's more a ladder than steps to get to the top. Not a good place to climb with a little kid. Herry won't go up there."

"Who's Herry?"

"My dog. The one you made the sandwich for."

"Oh, yeah. Looks like a bear." He let Dusty slide to the floor, where he stood clutching Zander's knee and now staring at Mandy. Zander scowled at the plastic-enclosed diaper. "I've got to figure out a way to get some diapers. I only had time to grab one package of them, and they won't last long."

"No babies at our house," Mandy said. "We could maybe borrow some dish towels. Or hand towels. I don't know if my mom would want us to use the dish towels. But we don't have enough of anything to last very long. I don't think you should stay here. Those guys are bound to find you before long. Were you serious about them not letting you live if they catch up with you?"

"Absolutely. Dusty's too little to tell anybody about them, so maybe they'll really give him back when Dad pays the ransom, but they wouldn't dare let me talk to the cops."

"We have to call the police," Mandy asserted. She knew that was what her parents would advise.

"I can't. Not until there's somebody around who believes me and will wait until my dad comes back from Japan. Kirby's a creep, but he puts on a good front when he's conning somebody. I've heard him working on Carol when he wants something, and he can be really smooth. Makes his ideas sound reasonable when he wants to cheat your socks off. And he *is* a lawyer, he knows how to talk to cops."

"Wouldn't you rather trust the cops to figure it out than take a chance on what Kirby will do if he catches you?"

Zander's consideration was brief. "No. I'm afraid of

them both. You don't know what I've been through. Did *you* believe me when I said I kidnapped my little brother to save him from *real* kidnappers?"

"I do now, since I've heard your story," Mandy said.

"Well, a slick lawyer is going to carry more weight with the cops than a kid too young to drive legally who swiped a car and took off with a little kid and then wrecked the car. I just have to find a place to stay out of sight until my dad comes home."

"And do you know when he's going to do that?"

"If he sticks to the original schedule, he should be home Monday." Zander looked at her hopefully as Dusty wandered off to pick up the graham cracker box that had fallen over on the end of the couch. "That's not all that long. If you can help me."

"But they're going to know you can't have gone far, lugging a little kid and his diapers. There's only your great-grandma's cottage and our house where you could have gone."

"It's a big house. You could hide us somewhere in it, couldn't you?"

"They've come there looking for you already. They wanted to talk to my folks. I didn't tell them I was there alone, but I'm pretty sure they suspected it. If they really want you, and they figure there's nobody else home—not too hard to do when there are no cars in the yard—what's to stop them breaking in to look for you?"

"We'd have a better chance than if we were in the woods, or out on the beach."

Mandy saw desperation on Zander's face. The idea of trying to conceal a fugitive from a couple of would-be kidnappers was scary, though, and she hesitated.

"You've got a phone, right? So if they come around again and get aggressive, we could call for help?"

"It'd make more sense to call now, before they come back. What if they cut the wires so we couldn't call?"

Dusty had sat down on the floor and was munching on a graham cracker. He really was cute, Mandy thought.

"But if the cops move in while my dad is still in Japan, where nobody can reach him, that smarmy Kirby is going to convince them he should have custody of us. That I'm a liar and can't be trusted."

There was something that flickered in Zander's face, and Mandy felt herself tightening up a little. "Are you? A liar? If the police try to call your home and ask, will somebody say you can't be trusted?"

"I don't know if they'll even get anybody if they call our place."

"What happened to the babysitter, Carol? Do you know? Would she vouch for you?"

Zander's tongue snaked over his lips. "I don't know. I don't know if Carol's still there. I mean, she insisted she wouldn't help them. I don't think she'd turn in her own brother. I think she might just do the same as I did. Run away."

"And if she's still there? Could you count on her to back you up?"

"I . . . I don't think she's still there."

"Did you see her leave?"

"Not . . . exactly."

Mandy made a strangled sound. "What does that mean? Why do I have the feeling you're fudging somehow? What aren't you telling me?"

"Look, I was scared, and I pulled Dusty out of his crib and grabbed the diaper bag and ran, okay? I don't know for sure what happened to Carol."

Mandy felt a suffocating chill run through her. "You left her there with two guys you think might murder you to keep you from testifying against them? While she was yelling she wouldn't cooperate in kidnapping your little brother?"

Zander stared at her, his jaw sagging, distress on his face. "What else could I have done?"

"Called the cops? There must have been a phone somewhere you could get at it."

"Not without them hearing me, or coming upstairs to get Dusty. All I could think of was to get out before they caught us!"

"And if they decided to murder Carol to keep her from talking? Didn't you consider that?"

"Well, she's Kirby's *sister*. I didn't think he'd kill *her*."

Obviously this boy had never watched cop shows on TV, or read any mystery books. He'd never made up stories and tried to keep them as realistic as Mandy had, when her sister wasn't trying to throw fantasy elements into the plot.

"Don't you watch the news? Statistically," Mandy said, using one of her favorite arguments, because she had a head for remembering numbers, "most murders are committed by relatives of the victims. If he'd kill you to keep from getting caught, why would he hesitate to do something bad to shut up his sister? He doesn't want to go to prison for what he wanted to do, right? What would it matter which one of you turned him in? Even if you couldn't call 9-1-1 before you got away from the house with Dusty, couldn't you have stopped at the first pay phone and called? The cops could have gone and rescued Carol."

"I never thought of it. All I could think of was getting as far away as I could, as fast as I could. You don't know what it's like to be so scared you can't think straight."

Yes, she did. She had been scared she was going to drown, and terrified that Angel was going to die. Her sister had saved her from drowning—more than once, when they weren't being careful enough in the water—and there had been no fear worse than knowing her sister was dying and nobody was able to save her.

"I've been scared. But never of anything I could control by calling the police. This time we can call the police."

Zander's mouth twisted in despair. "I've already told you why I can't! The cops aren't going to believe me! Only my dad's going to be able to save me, if I can just hide until Monday, when he gets home!"

"Could we at least call now and find out if Carol is okay?"

His eyes suddenly filled with moisture. "You don't really think they did anything to her, do you?"

"Let's go over to my house and call. Find out. Then— unless she's perfectly all right and her brother and his friend have given up on the idea of kidnapping any- body—we can call the cops."

"They haven't given up! If they had, they'd never have followed us!"

Mandy chewed on her lower lip while she thought about that. "How *did* they follow you? You got here a lot earlier than they did."

"I don't know how they figured out where I went."

"Why did you come here?"

"I didn't know Great-Grandma Hodge had died. I

thought for sure she'd help. Hide Dusty, at least, and maybe both of us. Give me enough money to get on a bus and go out to San Francisco. I've got an uncle out there, I think."

"You *think*?" Mandy heard her voice rising incredulously. "You were going to get on a bus and go all the way across the country without even knowing for sure where your uncle *is*? Don't you have his address?"

"No, but I figured he'd be in the phone book. Kirby and Larry don't know anything about him. They wouldn't look for me there."

"Don't you know anybody who'd help you who's closer than California?"

"Sure. Around Detroit. That's where we live most of the time. But they do know most of the places I might go *there*. Our house there is locked up, and they'd come looking to see if I'd broken in or anything like that."

"Do you have a reputation for breaking into houses?"

Zander suddenly blushed bright red. He stuffed the plastic bag with the used diaper in it into the blue bag and stood up. "Come on. Let's get out of here before they show up and start looking around. Maybe you're right about trying to call Carol and see if she's okay."

Mandy didn't move. "You have broken into somewhere before," she accused.

"It was on a dare. Last year. Four of us from school

broke into a house where there was nobody home, just to prove we could do it. We didn't steal anything, but there was a silent alarm we didn't know about. The cops came and caught us just looking around. That's all we meant to do, look around."

"And you got arrested."

"They didn't put us in jail or anything. They called all our folks to come and get us, and they bawled us out and told us next time they *would* lock us up. Come on, let's get out of here. You go out first, and I'll hand Dusty out to you."

"I think maybe," Mandy said, "you're the stupidest boy I have ever met."

As she said it, she realized to her amazement that she was talking to Zander the same way she'd always talked to Angel. She'd never ever talked to anyone else that way. She had thought she never would again.

Zander was still flushed pink, but he didn't protest her words. He swept up his little brother in one arm, carried the diaper bag in the other hand, and herded Mandy toward the opened bedroom window.

Herry rose from his resting place on the ground near the washtub they'd used for a step, wagging his tail. Mandy didn't have time to bother with him, but turned around and accepted the small boy while Zander followed her out of the cottage.

"If you knew people in Detroit, aren't there any friends

there who would have helped you? The father of a buddy or somebody like that?"

She passed Dusty back to Zander, taking over the blue canvas bag, waiting for him to reply.

Zander headed toward the beach in the direction of town, to where the Sebold house was just out of sight. "I'm not exactly on good terms with the fathers of any of my buddies," he said grimly as Mandy fell into step with him. "They think I'm a troublemaker." He hesitated. "And a liar. I've learned my lesson, but you're right, I've had times of being stupid. Breaking into Pat Milliken's house to look at his trophies—"

"The football player? Pat Milliken, the halfback? That's whose house you broke into?"

"—and we only ate a little out of that big can of popcorn, I didn't think anybody'd notice, and I said we hadn't touched anything—"

Mandy stumbled in the loose sand and almost fell. "So you're a kidnapper, and a thief, and a housebreaker, and a liar who got caught. What else have you not told me?"

Dusty was squirming, and Zander put him down and let him run ahead. "Nothing. That's it. I heard them planning to kidnap Dusty, and I knew Dad would pay the ransom, but on TV the kidnappers are always warning the parents not to call in the cops, and then the police want to deliver the ransom, and I wasn't sure how Dad would react to all that. I didn't want to do anything that would have got Dusty hurt. Sometimes on TV the kidnap victims get hurt."

Wide awake now, Dusty took off at a run toward the bay, and they both lunged after him, with Zander snatching an arm just before the little boy hit the water. "No, come on, I'm going to have to hold your hand," he said.

Dusty protested, but Zander was stronger and sort of dragged him along.

"Why don't you just let him walk in the edge of the water?" Mandy suggested. "Kids like to be in the water."

That worked well enough, and then Mandy looked back and realized that all three of them were leaving tracks in the wet sand.

"If those guys come looking out here, they'll see where we went."

"Oh, crumb! Wait, I'll run back and get that old broom and wipe out the tracks. We'd better stay up on the loose sand where they won't show."

Mandy stood holding Dusty's hand while Zander took care of the tracks, realizing that she was halfway doubting again that anybody could have done the things the boy claimed. Was Zander, too, a storyteller? Had he made up most of this?

But there was the wrecked car in the woods, and two

men had come searching for him, and he definitely had a small boy in tow.

Perhaps Zander read some of her uncertainty in her face. "I'm sure not lying about anything now," he said. "I guess it was stupid not to worry about Carol, but he's her brother. The keys to all our cars are hanging on a hook in the hall, by the front door, and I grabbed the ones to the SUV. Dusty was beginning to wake up. I was afraid he'd make enough noise so they'd hear him before we got out of the house.

"My dad let me drive a couple of times, when it was just us, on a back road. I never went out in a car alone before. I knew I wasn't a good enough driver to have a chance of driving very far, for sure not two hundred and fifty miles to Detroit, through all kinds of traffic, even if I had a place to hide from them when I got there. I hoped they'd think I'd try to go home, only I didn't dare."

Dusty was diverted by something on the ground—a feather from a seagull—and squatted to rescue it. Zander scooped him up to carry him. "I remembered Great-Grandma Hodge was on the other side of the bay, and late at night like that there wasn't much traffic until I got all the way to Traverse City. I sort of sweat blood getting through there, but at two in the morning I made it through town and kept coming out this way. I only saw one patrol car in Traverse, and I drove real carefully. He didn't pay any attention to me."

"How come you ran off the road and into a tree if you were able to drive well enough to come through Traverse City?" It wasn't a terribly big town, but much larger than Suttons Bay. When Rude was ten he had tried driving their dad's pickup and had run into a telephone pole, but if Zander had gotten all the way around the bottom of the bay and a town or two, what had caused a problem on their deserted road in the dark?

"A deer ran across in front of me. I wasn't going very fast, only about twenty miles an hour, when the darned thing ran right into the road in front of me and stopped. Like he was paralyzed when my headlights hit him, you know? I swerved to keep from hitting him and right about then I blew a tire and went off the road and hit the tree. Dusty smacked his head and started to cry."

"You didn't have him buckled in?" Mandy demanded.

"You really do think I'm an idiot, don't you? I didn't have time to get his car seat, and he was back to sleep by the time I laid him down in the front seat, and I did the best I could to get a belt around him. It wasn't a very good job, I guess, but I never dared to stop and fix it, for fear they were chasing me."

"And now we're back to how they guessed you'd come here."

Zander sighed. Dusty dropped his seagull feather and squirmed, complaining, to get down and retrieve it.

Mandy picked it up and handed it to him, tickling him under the chin with it before handing it over. Dusty had a charming smile.

"I don't know. All I know is I can't let them catch me before my dad comes." Zander stopped abruptly, tilting his head. "Do you hear a car?"

Faintly, in the distance, an engine could be heard.

"Yes." Mandy had a moment of hope that some member of her family was returning early. "Maybe my folks—"

"It sounds like that old van of Kirby's," Zander said, and he broke into a trot, heading for the shelter of the woods.

⮜ 10 ⮞

Mandy's heart was suddenly racing. The diaper bag slapped against her leg as she ran after Zander into the edge of the woods.

The sound of the car was nearer now, and by the time they'd reached her house, there was no doubt that the vehicle had pulled into her own driveway. They stopped, both of them winded, hearing the car doors slam as the men got out.

Blood thundered in Mandy's ears, almost drowning out Zander's words as she sucked in a breath.

"Cripes! It's them, I know it's them! I know the sound of that car, it's losing a rod, hear it?"

Mandy didn't know anything about the sounds that would be made if a car were losing a rod. "They got out of the car. They're going to the house. Maybe when they knock and nobody comes, they'll just go away."

"They've figured out I have to be close by," Zander said, shifting Dusty to his other arm.

In the silence a gull screamed, diving on something that had washed up on the shore. When the intruders knocked loudly, Mandy jumped. Both of them moved farther into the trees, trying to hide behind the nearer ones, but most were not big enough or thick enough in their lower branches to conceal them very well. Herry, compliant as he usually was, stopped when Mandy did, close enough that she could scratch behind his ear. She didn't think to do it.

Zander began to inch along, closer to the house. That was all right as long as his pursuers stayed near the back door, but what if they came around the corner?

"Nobody home," one of the men stated. "Either that, or the girl's not gonna answer the door."

"We'd better go in and check the place out," the other guy said. "See if there's any sign of that brat. He wrecked the car, and he's dragging Dusty along with him, he's not gonna be able to run very far. He's gotta go to ground somewhere."

So at least part of Zander's story was accurate. She hadn't even locked up the house when she left, so they wouldn't have to break into it.

"It's open," one of the men said. "Come on, let's take a look. Might find something worth taking."

"What're we gonna do if the girl's here?" the other voice asked.

The screen door slammed loudly, and the watchers outside could no longer hear their voices.

Indignation boiled through Mandy. This was no made-up story, and Angel wasn't around to help with a solution. But they'd walked right into her house, and though she hadn't heard the reply to the question of what they would do to her if they found her, the possibilities made her break out in a cold sweat. How dare they rob her house!

"Let's make a run for it," Zander broke into her thoughts, "and steal their car while they're in the house."

She blinked, staring at him. "Are you crazy? You can't even drive!"

"I drove well enough to get here from the other side of the bay, didn't I? If it wasn't for that stupid deer jumping in front of me, I wouldn't have run off the road. Come on, let's go for it while they're searching the house."

"What if the keys aren't in it and they come out and see us?"

"The keys are probably in it. Kirby's a careless kind of guy. Let's go, before they come back out!"

"Probably. Probably! But maybe not! Even if the key is

in it, the minute you start the engine they'll hear it and come tearing out to stop us!"

"But they don't have any way to chase us. If the motor's running, and we lock the doors, we can get out of the yard without them being able to stop us."

"What if they jump on the hood, or get in our way?"

"We'll run over them. Or leave 'em on the hood and get going fast enough so they'll fall off," Zander said, as if that were perfectly logical.

"What if they have guns? If they shoot out the tires, we won't get very far."

"I don't know if Kirby would have a gun," Zander said, but at least he seemed to be thinking about the possibility.

"But you don't know that for sure, either. How did you think they would shut you up—kill you—if they weren't prepared to shoot you?"

"You talk funny, you know? Like you're reading from a book," Zander said.

Mandy gave up. "We can't get in the house to use the phone. We can't try to call Carol. The only sensible thing to do is to stay out of sight until they're gone, and then call the cops. They won't let Kirby do anything to you. We just need to hide somewhere until it's safe for us to come back."

"Okay. Where?" Zander asked.

When voices became audible, only yards away

through the window Mandy had left open, they both jumped. Dusty made a small protesting sound, and Zander put a hand over his mouth. "Shhh! We're playing hide and seek, remember how we do that? You don't make any noise!"

Dusty stuck out his lower lip, but he didn't speak.

Inside the house someone asked, "Did you hear something?"

"No. Look, you go upstairs and check everything out. I'll finish searching this floor. Hurry! The girl left the place wide open, so she's not going to be gone for long."

"We already found a little cash and a laptop. Maybe we should forget the upstairs."

"Go!"

"So what're you gonna do with the girl if she shows up? We wasn't supposed to *kill* anybody, just snatch the kid and get the ransom money."

At that point the men had moved away from the window, and though their voices could still be detected, their words could not.

Mandy wished, while not really wanting to have her fears confirmed, that she'd heard more. The chill caused by that question about *killing* her was paralyzing.

Herry nudged her hand and swished his tail, suggesting that she pay more attention to him. Absently her fingers massaged behind his ear. Much as she loved him, at this moment she'd have traded him for a vicious watchdog.

Zander's whisper sounded too loud in the echoing silence around them. "They're searching now. I'm going to jump in the car and run."

"Run where? I thought you were willing to go to the cops now. What if they catch us?"

"We'll split up," Zander considered, not answering her concerns. "I'll run for the car, and you hide with Dusty, so if they catch me you'll still be free to get help. If they catch me, you can still call the cops."

"And where am I supposed to hide Dusty? For how long? If you take their car, who knows how long they'll hang around, watching for us."

"They won't stay here, once they see their car's gone. They'll figure out I took it. They'll hightail it out of here, find another car, get out of town before the cops might chase them."

"But you're convinced they won't take the chance that you might report them to the police! Zander, they're talking about *killing* people!"

He'd already considered that and it seemed he didn't want to think about it any further. "I'm going to make a run for the car. You coming with me, or are you going to hide Dusty?"

Where? There was no good hiding place. No safety in

the old cannery, or the lighthouse, or even the place the boys had built in the woods. No way to get to any of them quickly, carrying a two-year-old who quickly grew too heavy.

Mandy inhaled deeply, exhaled. It didn't make her head any clearer.

She could not hear the men talking. Presumably that meant they were deeply into searching the house.

She had a momentary vision of her parents returning and finding her dead in the middle of the yard. It wasn't nearly as easy to think about as it would have been if she'd been making up a story.

"Doggy," Dusty said suddenly, stretching down to reach Herry. "Play with doggy."

"No, buddy," Zander said.

"I'm not keeping him by myself," Mandy said.

"Then we'll both run. Stay as close to me as you can, and when I get a door open, pile in. I'll carry Dusty and hand him to you as soon as you're inside."

As far as Mandy could see, there was no other option. She'd have been happier if Zander's judgments had been better in the past, but there was no way to change that. Maybe he'd be right about something once in a while. She hoped this was the time.

Zander ran before she was ready. He rounded the corner of the house and set off across the open space to the car, grabbing for the handle of the rear door on the near side, jerking it open and stepping out of her way.

Mandy practically flung herself onto the backseat, immediately twisted to accept Dusty.

Zander slammed the door—would they hear that from inside the house?—and opened the door into the driver's seat.

Everybody had forgotten about Herry.

He had, naturally, joined them in the dash across the yard. Now he practically knocked Zander off his feet, leaping past him into the front seat.

For a few seconds Mandy didn't realize what the dog was doing, pawing at something encased in a plastic bag on the seat. And then she smelled it. Unmistakable. Peanut butter.

Zander piled in behind Herry, having to take time to shove the massive dog out of his way, but before he could even slam the door behind him, the men erupted from the back door of the house. One of them carried the Sebolds' laptop computer.

"Stop, you little creep!" That was Larry, stumbling on the steps and nearly falling. He put the computer down.

Kirby didn't stumble. He raced toward them, his face thunderous, and grabbed the handle on the open car door so Zander couldn't close it.

Mandy glanced past Zander at the ignition, where

Zander had thought there would probably be keys left behind by a careless Kirby.

There were no keys.

The only sound was Herry tearing at the plastic bag, then gulping at the sandwich it had contained.

"We're gonna have to kill the dog, too," Larry gasped, having finally arrived right behind his co-conspirator.

Mandy's chest tightened, her breath catching painfully.

She formed an almost wordless prayer. This would be a wonderful time for her parents to come home. They'd know what to do. Wouldn't they? She had complete faith in Mom and Dad.

But nobody came.

Please, God, help, Mandy thought desperately.

There was no heavenly response. Just Herry, swallowing audibly, and the smell of peanut butter.

⤳ 11 ⤳

"Samwich," Dusty said.

He leaned forward, over Mandy's arm, reaching for the back of the front seat and the big dog who was just swallowing the last of his find in the plastic bag he'd torn open.

"Hungry," Dusty said.

He did not appear to be alarmed at the appearance of Kirby and Larry, whom he had presumably seen before at home. Nor did he seem aware of Zander and Mandy's fright.

"She was right about taming the kid with a peanut butter sandwich," Larry said angrily, "but the dang dog ate it."

Kirby sounded cold and angry. "I didn't notice you leaping in and taking it away from him."

Having devoured the food, Herry was now wagging his tail, but the two men never noticed.

"Planning to leave, were you?" Kirby asked. "Without the keys?" He pulled them out of his pants pocket and jangled them in front of Zander.

Zander stuck out his chin. "I thought for sure you'd be stupid enough to leave them in the ignition."

Mandy sucked in a breath. Why was this idiot boy deliberately antagonizing the man? Weren't they in enough trouble already?

"Come on," Larry said angrily, "let's get out of here before anybody else shows up. What are we gonna do with these brats?"

"More than likely," Kirby said without a trace of humor, "they are going to have an accident. How do you suggest we get that critter out of the front seat?"

"It belongs to the girl. She oughta be able to make it get out," Larry said.

"Okay. Tell it to get out," Kirby told her, staring at Mandy.

Her mouth was dry. She didn't know anything to do except comply with the order, so she tried. "Herry, get out of the car."

Herry glanced at her over the back of the seat, tail waving gently. This was not one of the commands with which he was familiar. His peanut-buttery breath wafted toward her.

Mandy glanced at the man still nervously juggling his keys. "I'll have to get out, and then call him out."

"So do it," he said, and jerked the back door wide open.

In climbing out, leaving Dusty behind, Mandy tripped over the diaper bag, kicking it out onto the ground.

It had not been zipped closed the last time it was used, and its contents spilled onto the sand. Disposable diapers, a milky bottle, a crumbled graham cracker. And something else nobody would have expected to be there.

A twisted tangle of glittery objects that Mandy instantly recognized as jewelry.

She'd never seen anything but costume jewelry, because that was all her mother had, but she had a hunch this stuff was more expensive. Like real gold, and real silver and turquoise, and probably genuine pearls. Beautiful stuff, including a ring with a stone that might be a diamond sparkling in the sunlight.

Larry let out a muffled exclamation as he made a dive for the pile, bringing up both hands full of necklaces, pins, and bracelets. He'd missed the ring, and Kirby grabbed for it, grimacing.

"Why, you little creep!" he said to Zander, and for a moment Mandy thought he was going to strike the boy. "No wonder we couldn't find this stuff."

She felt like hitting him herself. What else hadn't he

told her, besides the fact that in addition to kidnapping his little brother, he had also swiped his stepmother's jewelry?

No doubt the conspirators had intended to confiscate that as well as ask for a ransom for the little boy.

Larry looked as indignant as if the jewelry had belonged to him. Once they'd decided to steal it, perhaps he felt as if it did.

Mandy had fallen to a knee but managed to get back on her feet. "What are you going to do with us?" she demanded, hating the fact that her voice squeaked.

Instead of answering that, Kirby scowled. "Get your dog out of the car."

Swallowing hard, Mandy snapped her fingers at her pet. "Come on, Herry. Get out."

He understood "come." He leaped past Zander, out of the vehicle. Both men hastily backed up to get out of his way, though the dog showed no inclination to attack either of them. Unfortunately. To Herry, everybody was a friend who might provide a treat.

"Slide over," Kirby told Zander, and got into the driver's seat before the boy could even move to obey. He had the keys in his hand and slammed the door at once to make sure Herry couldn't reenter.

"What about me?" Larry demanded, backing a little farther away from Herry, who was sniffing at Mandy's hand.

"Get in the back. Put the girl in with you," Kirby said crossly. Visions of various possible "accidents" flitted through Mandy's mind. *Oh, Mom and Dad, please come home!*

Larry pushed her back into the rear seat with Dusty.

She picked up the scattered items from the diaper bag and thrust it ahead of her into the limited space. She bumped the back of Zander's head with it, but he didn't act as if he'd felt it, and he didn't say anything.

Considering how stupid some of what he'd said had been, maybe that was just as well.

Larry hauled himself inside, closed the door when Herry poked his nose toward him, and wheezed out a stressed breath. "Let's get out of here," he said.

Kirby put the car in gear, backed it around, and headed out of the driveway. There were no other cars on the road as they headed toward town.

Halfway there, Larry turned and looked out the rear window and let out an explosive huff. "He's following us! The danged dog is following us! Go faster! Lose him!"

The car lurched forward under Kirby's increased foot pressure. "Don't worry about him. He can't keep up."

Mandy couldn't bring herself to turn and look. Poor Herry. He probably thought there were more sandwiches somewhere if he could catch up to them.

Maybe, Mandy thought desperately, they'd see someone

going through the village, someone she could flag down or signal about their plight. Maybe even a police car.

But already, before they were in the middle of the little town, Kirby was turning off. Up the slight grade, stopping at the Bay View, the only motel in Suttons Bay.

Mandy knew the people who owned it—Mr. and Mrs. Olsson—just as she knew everyone else in town. But there was no sign of either of them, nor of any other guests, as the car slid into a parking slot in front of the door numbered 8.

Kirby jerked the keys free and jammed them in his pocket. "Inside, everybody inside."

There was nothing to do but obey. Larry pointed at Dusty. "Bring him," he said harshly to Mandy.

She scooped him up, and allowed herself to be herded into the motel room.

She'd never been in it, and was surprised at how small it was, and how crowded once they'd gotten inside. Dusty felt disgusting, and when he squirmed, she let him slide to the floor. The minute she let go of him, he squealed and ran across the room to the young woman sitting in a chair at a small table.

"Caro," he cried in delight.

"Carol?" Zander echoed. There was no doubting his bewilderment and shock.

Equally confused, Mandy could only stare.

The babysitter was in her mid-twenties, a sun-bleached blonde in jeans and a print shirt. She gathered up the little boy in a bear hug, ignoring his messy state. "Hi, little buddy. Did you miss me?"

Kirby had closed the door behind them. The window shades were drawn, and except for a pool of light from the lamp beside Carol, it was nearly dark in the room. Mandy stood uncertainly, while Zander figured it out ahead of her.

Carol's brother had not harmed her to keep her from turning them over to the police. She had joined them in their robbery/kidnapping scheme.

"You were in on it with them," Zander blurted, incredulous. "You're just as guilty as they are!"

"I hoped you'd have sense enough to mind your own business," Carol said, looking directly at him. "I should have known better."

"But I heard you! They were telling you they were going to hold Dusty for ransom, and you told them you wouldn't be part of it! You wouldn't jeopardize your job, and you cared about Dusty!"

"I do care about Dusty. Nothing bad is going to happen to him. He's too little to tell anybody what's going on."

The implied threat—*you're not too little to tell*—hung in the air in the room that was suddenly too close to allow

Mandy to breathe easily. She tried to suck in a fresh gulp of air and felt dizzy enough to fall down.

"He met this girl," Larry started to explain. "She hid him. So we had to bring her along."

Carol looked at Zander as if she were genuinely sorry he was involved. "It would have been a lot easier if you'd just stayed out of it. We knew you were listening outside the kitchen door, we heard you coming. Your feet are so big you sound like an elephant. So we talked loud enough to make sure you could hear us. I thought you'd run and hide, then call the cops after Kirby and Larry were gone with Dusty and swear I had nothing to do with any of it when they came." She smiled a little, ever sadder. "Now look what you've gotten yourself into."

"What?" Zander asked. "You can just give Dusty back, and go away and forget the whole thing. Nobody's been hurt."

"Yet," Carol said, and there was silence from the men. A deadly silence.

Because they couldn't afford to just let Mandy and Zander and Dusty free. Not when two of them could testify to what they'd been through, what the plan had been. Even planning a kidnapping was illegal, wasn't it? And they'd tried to rob Mandy's house.

Mandy stood frozen, her heart hammering the way it had the time she'd been close to swallowing enough water to drown, if her sister hadn't grabbed her by the hair and held her face out of the water long enough for her to get a grip on the edge of the boat.

Carol and her brother and his friend were going to kill her and Zander.

They wouldn't do it in front of Dusty, would they? He couldn't talk very well, but surely he would be badly frightened if he saw such a thing happening. Could they count on his silence if he were a witness?

"Take the kid somewhere else," Kirby said.

Carol took Dusty's hand. "Come on, kiddo, we're going to take a walk."

Mandy's gaze locked with Zander's. He realized what this meant too. He swallowed convulsively.

If he were her sister, they would have passed a message between them. *We have to both explode into action at the same time. Surprise them enough to get out of here before they can act to hurt us.*

Did Zander get that?

Carol stepped rapidly toward the door and pulled it open.

And stopped because a police car was just pulling in behind Kirby's van, blocking its way.

Mandy didn't know why it was there, but she screamed "Help!" as loud as she could and leaped for the doorway before Carol had passed through it. So did

Zander, knocking Carol down, spilling Dusty onto the sidewalk. Mandy fell forward onto her hands and knees beside Carol, feeling grit cutting into her palms.

And suddenly Herry was licking Mandy's cheek, and Uncle Frank was protesting to the officer who had gotten out of the patrol car.

"I didn't do anything! I never hurt the tomatoes, and when he told me to get out of the store, I did it! I was just following the dog, because he's not supposed to be in town without being on a leash! He's not my dog, anyway, so he's not my responsibility, but I was just going to take him home!"

Mandy knew the officer. His name was Clancy, and he hitched up his gun belt, because it kept sliding down beneath his belly.

"Help us!" Mandy blurted, hooking an arm around Herry's neck to hold him off. "They're kidnappers! They're going to kill us so we can't tell on them!" Her heart was pounding so hard she could barely hear her own voice.

Clancy scowled and held up a hand to signify that she should be quiet. He reached for the clip-on radio at his collar. "Clancy here, I'm at the Bay View Motel in Suttons Bay, need backup, Code Ten." He suddenly rested his hand on the butt of his gun. "Ah, ah, raise your hands up over your heads, and step through the doorway. Don't make any other move until I say you can, or I'll sic the dog on you."

He was obviously speaking to Kirby and Larry. Carol was still sprawled on the sidewalk, and Dusty was heading toward Zander, undecided whether to cry or not.

Whether it was the threat of the gun or of Herry was not clear, but the men offered no resistance. Their confident attitude had dissolved entirely.

"Now," Clancy said, "tell me what's going on."

"These kids kidnapped the baby I was babysitting," Carol asserted, pushing herself into a sitting position. "My brother was trying to rescue us."

"She's a liar," Zander interjected frantically. "He's my little brother!"

Uncle Frank said, "Is that the real Mandy or the other one?"

The gun swung between Zander and Carol, then back to Larry and Kirby, who twitched ever so slightly. "Code Ten, before I have to shoot somebody!" Clancy barked into the radio again. And then, sounding increasingly irritated, "SHUT UP!"

A new voice entered the ensuing silence as Ray Olsson, the motel owner, stuck his head out of the office door at the end of the unit. "What's going on? Clancy, what's up?"

"That's what I'm trying to find out. Call 911, will you,

Ray, and tell them I need backup, Code Ten. If the rest of these yahoos will keep still, I hope Mandy can tell me if I stepped into the middle of a crime here."

Mandy drew a deep breath. "Yes, sir. Those men tried to kidnap Dusty, the baby, only Zander overheard them and took him first. They followed him and said they were going to kill Zander and me so we couldn't turn them in."

"Nobody's going to kill anybody," Clancy said, and never in all the years she'd known him had he sounded so menacing. "Ray, would you step over here until my backup comes, and just make sure these gentlemen are not carrying weapons? They're going to keep their hands up, and don't get between them and me, okay? Go around behind them."

The motel proprietor, looking decidedly uneasy, hesitated. "Shall I go call 911 first? Or search them?"

"Search them," Clancy decided. And then, as the radio near his throat chattered, he said into it, "Ten four," quite forcefully. "My backup's on the way, Ray, so you don't need to call. Will somebody take care of that baby before he wanders off?"

Zander stepped quickly forward and scooped up his little brother.

"Don't get in my line of fire!" Clancy said crossly. He wasn't used to this much stress, and it was making him short-tempered. The closest he'd ever been to a kidnapping before, Mandy learned later, was reading about one in the newspaper.

"Neither of 'em has a gun. This one had a pocket knife," Ray said, stepping cautiously away from the men he'd searched. He displayed it on his hand. "Here's his car keys."

"Okay. Hang onto them. Now, you two, drop on the ground with your hands above your heads and stay that way. Mandy, go with Ray to the office telephone and call your folks."

"They're in Traverse City."

"Then call your aunt, or one of your brothers."

Her heart was pounding, but she could hear better now. Did she imagine it, or was there the faint wail of a siren in the distance? Maybe one of the sheriff's deputies had been close enough to get the message already.

She turned to follow Mr. Olsson toward the office.

No matter what happened now, Clancy wasn't going to let anyone hurt her or Zander.

She glanced back and saw Carol, rubbing at an elbow she'd scraped when she fell, glaring at Zander, and then, swiftly, at her.

For a moment the hatred and resentment she saw in the young woman's face were chilling. Zander had thought she was a victim too, of her brother and Larry, but she would willingly have sacrificed anybody for gain; she'd deliberately misled Zander into thinking she was a pawn, and presumably if she'd gotten away with it she would have shared in the ransom and the value of the stolen jewelry and gone on with her job of babysitting Dusty.

Struck by sudden puzzlement, Mandy hesitated. Encouraged by the presence of an armed police officer, she demanded, "How did you know where Zander had gone? You didn't follow him from home or you'd have been here earlier."

"Yeah," Zander backed her, "I didn't even know where I was going when I left home, so how did you figure it out?"

Carol's sneer made Mandy wonder how anyone could have thought she was the type of person they wanted to take care of their precious little boy.

"I suppose it never occurred to you that your mother's old address book was still in the desk drawer in the dining room, did it? Nobody ever got rid of it after she died. And her grandmother's address was still in it. She lived the closest to where we were, and it seemed like a logical place to head for. I knew you couldn't drive well enough to go very far. I'm surprised you made it here without wrecking the car sooner."

She spoke with contempt—for Zander, for Mandy, for everybody—but Mandy wondered how defiant she would be when she was forced to appear in court, with Zander testifying against her. The consequences of being part of a kidnapping conspiracy would be severe.

Mandy jumped when Herry's cold nose poked into her hand, and she automatically moved to scratch behind his ears. Good old Herry! He'd followed after the car that carried them away, and Uncle Frank had spotted him and pursued him, and then Clancy had been curious enough to trail Uncle Frank here to the motel. She shuddered, refusing to think what would have happened if he'd been a few minutes later. Her own lunge toward freedom might easily have failed if Clancy had not followed Herry and Uncle Frank at exactly the right time.

Who said God doesn't answer prayers, even the frantic, incoherent ones that were all she'd been able to muster in the past few hours? He'd been working it all out from the beginning.

And Mandy's own brain—apart from the mind of Angel, on which she had depended so heavily for all of her life—had kept her going through things wilder than her imagination had ever produced.

Mr. Olsson dialed Aunt Eileen's phone number. "Frank and Mandy are here at the motel," he said when she answered. "Everything's fine now, but I need to get hold of Mandy's folks right away." After a brief pause, he said, "I'll explain it all later. Just give me the number."

He scribbled the number, hung up, then dialed again before handing the phone to Mandy.

Two minutes later she heard her father's voice over the wires.

"It's me, Daddy, Mandy. I think you better come home right away. Everything's okay, but I'm at the Bay View Motel, and Clancy's here, and we'll tell you everything when you get here, all right?"

And Dad, bless him, accepted that tidbit without demanding details over the phone. "We're coming," he said, and hung up.

When she turned back to the door, Zander stood there with Dusty on his hip.

"The other cop is here," he announced. "I think they want us all to go back to the police station." He swallowed hard. "You'll tell them I didn't do anything illegal, won't you?"

Nothing but rescue Dusty by kidnapping him first, swiping an SUV he couldn't legally drive, and break into the Sebold house to help himself to groceries. Oh, yeah, and he took his stepmother's jewelry to keep it out of Kirby's hands.

"When my parents get here," Mandy said, finally relaxing, "I'll tell them everything."

And right then, walking out into the motel parking lot where there were now two police cars, Mandy began thinking up the contribution that her sister would be making if she were here, and she knew that never, ever would she be completely without Angel again.

"One more thing," she said to Zander, "why were you watching TV when you broke into our house? There aren't even any stations on in the middle of the night."

Zander was obviously shaken, but he had the grace to look chastened. "I thought maybe I'd get a newscast, find out if anybody was chasing me. In Detroit we can get news all night long. I'm sorry I scared you."

"I wasn't really scared," Mandy said untruthfully. "I just couldn't figure out why the TV was turned on."

She knew she'd have been a lot more scared, though, if she hadn't been able to figure out what her sister would have done and said in similar circumstances. And she was pretty sure that from now on, even all by herself, she would be able to lean on what Angel would have thought or said. Because she knew Angel that well. Nobody would ever be able to change that.

"I'm not under arrest, am I?" Uncle Frank asked loudly. "I didn't do anything."

Clancy rested a hand on Frank's shoulder. "No, you're not under arrest. But we're all going to have to sit down at the station and answer some questions and get some answers. Guess we better take the dog in the car with Mandy and me, right?"

Uncle Frank was nodding vigorously as he climbed in behind her. "You tell your ma, it's not against the law to talk to tomatoes."

A smile began to loosen up her face and she squeezed his hand as they sat down next to each other in the back of the police car.

"I'll be sure to tell her, Uncle Frank," she said.